A HARD WELCOME

Mitch was halfway back to town when he found the road blocked by four mounted men. Each man had the look of a hard ruffian. Each man had a stern expression on his face. One man held a shotgun at the ready. Mitch moved his horse over close to the mountain wall which rose high above, in order to make room for the riders to pass him by on the narrow road. None of them made a move.

"You got something on your mind?" Mitch asked.

"Yeah," said one of the riders, a large man with a red beard. "You."

"What about me?" Mitch said.

"We want you out of town," the red beard said.

"I can't do that," said Mitch. "I've got a job."

"You can quit your job and ride out," said the red beard. "There's folks in Paxton who don't take kindly to having a damned Apache with a badge lording it over them."

"Is that right?" Mitch said. "What folks would they be? You four?"

"Us four," said the red beard, "and others."

"Take it up with the mayor," said Mitch. "Right now, get out of my way."

The man with the shotgun moved it slightly so that it was leveled at Mitch. Mitch knew that there was no arguing with a shotgun.

"We'll get out of your way," the red beard said, "after we've done a little convincing on you."

Apache Law

The Lonely Gun

LUKE ADAMS

LEISURE BOOKS   NEW YORK CITY

A LEISURE BOOK®

November 1999

Published by

Dorchester Publishing Co., Inc.
276 Fifth Avenue
New York, NY 10001

ISBN 0-8439-4631-8

Apache Law

The Lonely Gun

Chapter One

Mitch Frye lounged in the shade of the canteen directly across from the Arizona headquarters of the Sixth Cavalry at Fort Apache. He was sitting in the dirt beside another civilian scout, Tom Horn, leaning back against the adobe wall of the canteen. Al Sieber, chief of scouts, was inside the office with General Nelson Miles, newly arrived as a replacement for General Crook. The Apache scouts waited in a group not far away. No one was talking. None of the scouts, white civilian or Apache, was happy with the news that Crook had been replaced. They knew Crook well and respected him. Most of them had been with him for the last four years. None of them was happy with his replacement. They accepted it, though. They had to. There was nothing they could do about it.

General Crook had been in command of the Sixth Cavalry and in charge of the Geronimo campaign since 1882. After four years, General Phil Sheridan, Commander of the Division of the Missouri, had lost his patience with Crook's failure to confine Geronimo and his followers to the reservation. It was well known that Sheridan did not approve of Crook's use of Apache scouts and did not, in fact, think too highly even of any civilian scouts. Geronimo's last breakout had been the last straw for Sheridan, an advocate of total warfare and a faithful disciple of William Tecumseh Sherman. He blamed the Apache scouts, and he blamed Crook for having trusted them. So Crook was out and Miles was in, and the scouts, white civilian and Apache alike, all anxiously but patiently awaited news of their fates.

Mitch Frye rolled himself a smoke. He tucked the makings back into his shirt pocket, withdrew a wooden match from the same pocket, struck it on the side of the building, and held the flame to his cigarette. He puffed and watched the smoke slowly drift away in the hot desert air. Following the drift of the smoke, he glanced toward the Apache scouts off to his left, their faces betraying no emotion, no concern. He knew they were worried, though. They'd heard the talk. They were good men, all of them. In a way, he thought, they were much like him, but in other ways nothing like him at all. He often felt as if there was no one in the world like himself. Mitch was more comfortable with the likes of Sieber and Horn than with the scouts, the reservation Apaches, the soldiers, or the white people in the nearby towns, but he never really felt quite at home, never felt quite like he belonged anywhere.

"You reckon old stiff-pants is going to keep Al in there all day?" Tom Horn said, breaking the long silence.

Mitch only shrugged. Then he pulled the makings out of his pocket again and held them toward Horn, who accepted them, rolled himself a smoke, and handed them back to Mitch. Horn lit his smoke just as the office door across the way opened up, and he said, "Here he comes now." As Sieber walked over toward them, the two civilian scouts stood up to meet him. "Well?" Horn asked.

"Well, boys," said Sieber, "it seems the Army don't need our services no more."

"We're cut loose?" said Horn.

"That's right," Sieber said. "Miles and Sheridan both agree that Crook relied too much on scouts. Not just Apaches, all of us. They believe that the Army can do the job right—without us."

"How the hell can they trail Apaches without scouts?" Horn asked.

"They got their books on military tactics," Sieber answered wryly.

"Well, that's that," Horn said. He tossed away his cigarette only half smoked.

Frye said nothing, but he was wondering just what he would do with himself now. His job as a scout for the Sixth had given him the closest thing he had ever known to a home. Even while his mother had still been alive, and he had been at home with her, even then he had felt alone and unwanted, not unwanted by her but by everyone else around. He had never known a father, so when she died, he had been left completely alone. Horn and Sieber were the only men he had ever known who didn't seem to care about his background.

"What're you going to do, Al?" Horn asked.

"Get drunk, I guess," Sieber said.

"Seems like as good a plan as any," Horn agreed.

"When I sober up," Sieber added, "I'll worry then about what to do next. I'll find something. Hell, I always have. What about you?"

"I'll join you, at least for the drinking part, if you don't mind," said Horn.

"Suit yourself," Sieber said. "We'll ride down to Tucson." Then he looked at Mitch. "What about you?"

"I don't know, Al," said Mitch. "I got no place to go. I don't know what I'll do."

"It could be worse, kid," Sieber said. He glanced over at the Apache scouts, still waiting patiently for word on their status. "If that straitlaced son of a bitch in there finds out that you're half Apache, you'll be on your way to Florida with those poor bastards."

"He's sending the Apache scouts to Florida?" Horn said, incredulous.

"That's right," Sieber snarled, "along with all the rest of the residents of the San Carlos Reservation. Every last one of them."

"Hell," said Horn. "They've done good service. It ain't right."

"You know how Phil Sheridan thinks," Sieber said.

"Yeah," said Horn. "The son of a bitch."

"The only good Indian's a dead one," said Mitch in a quiet voice, echoing the famous comment attributed to Sheridan.

Sieber held out a handful of coins for Horn and then another for Mitch. "Severance pay, he called it," he said. "It'll buy us some whiskey over in Tucson. You coming along, Mitch?"

Mitch shrugged. "I reckon," he said.

"Right now," said Sieber, "I better go tell those poor devils over yonder about their fate. I'd rather be kicked by a mule."

Riding toward Tucson in the company of Al Sieber and Tom Horn, Mitch did a lot of thinking. He was all right with these two men. He was comfortable riding with them and when they camped for the night, but he had been to Tucson before, and his appearance had brought looks of anger and some angry words from the citizens there. He knew that he owed his features, his skin tone and hair color, more to his un-known Apache father than to his white mother, and he also knew that Arizona whites had nothing but hatred in their hearts for Apaches. Whatever happened, Sieber and Horn would stand with him against any odds. He knew that, too. Still, the thought of what could happen in Tucson troubled him.

They sat around their small fire just as the sun was rising over the distant hills, sipping their morning coffee. Another half day's ride would take them on into Tucson. The morning air and the silence were pleasant. The company of the only two men he had ever called friend in the solitude of the vast landscape was comforting. But the prospect of Tucson and its inhabitants by midday was unsettling to Mitch. He sipped hot coffee from a tin cup.

"Al," said Horn, "where do you think you'll go after Tucson?"

"I ain't give it a thought," Sieber answered. "I don't mean to do any thinking yet for a few days."

"I might go to mining," Horn said. "Gold or silver. It don't matter none. Wherever I can stake me a claim."

"That's too much like gambling for my taste," Sieber said. "And like I said, right now I ain't thinking beyond drinking."

"Hell, you're right," Horn said. "By God, I'll be drunk as a skunk, have me a whore, and pass clean out, all before dark."

"Not if we don't get started right away, you won't," said Sieber.

They put out their fire and packed their things into the blanket rolls that they carried behind their saddles. As they mounted up, Mitch turned his horse around to face north. "I guess I'll be seeing you," he said.

"Where you going?" said Horn.

"I think I'll just head back north," said Mitch. "I been thinking. I don't much like Tucson."

"Back to Fort Apache?" Horn asked.

"No," said Mitch. "Not there."

Al Sieber opened his mouth to speak, hesitated a moment, then said, "Take care of yourself, Mitch. After a few days of drinking to get the bad taste of old Miles out of my system, I'll light somewhere. If you ever need anything, look me up."

Mitch nodded, kicked his heels into his horse's sides, and rode off, leaving the other two former scouts behind. They watched him for a moment, then Sieber said, "Let's go," and they rode on toward Tucson with its whiskey and whores.

11

Mitch had no destination in mind other than north. That would take him farther away from the Apaches, from Tucson, and from the Sixth Cavalry. He had a few dollars in his pocket, his good horse, his saddle, a change of clothes, and most important, his Colt .45 Peacemaker, his Winchester rifle, and plenty of ammunition for both. He didn't know where he was going or what he was going to do, but he knew that he could take care of himself.

At first, of course, he was only retracing his own path. He had ridden south with Sieber and Horn and then decided to turn back north. He wasn't going back to Fort Apache or the vicinity of San Carlos, but to ride on north of that area, he would have to pass right through it. He didn't feel like he had wasted his time or his energy, though. He had no plans, and he had enjoyed a few more days of the company of his two friends. He'd likely have stayed on with them if they had been planning anything other than a visit to Tucson.

He made the return trip casually and with no incidents. He did a little hunting along the way, just enough to provide himself with fresh meat at his campfires, and when he reached the San Carlos area he rode a careful trail to avoid seeing anyone from the reservation or the fort who would know him. Eventually he reached the mountains to the north. He didn't know just how long he had been on the trail alone. He wasn't counting the days.

Sitting alone at his campfire one cold night, he pondered his possibilities. His few dollars wouldn't last long. He would have to make some kind of decision. He'd have to come up with some way of making a living. He considered buffalo hunting. It was still a possibility, although it wasn't what it used to be. The great buffalo herds had already been thinned considerably. He could do that, though, and make some money, and if he was careful with it and held on to most of it, it would hold him for a spell until he could think up something better.

It was an idea, and he didn't totally discard it. He didn't embrace it, either. Hide hunting, he thought, was a dirty business. The hide hunter killed as many beasts as he could in a day, skinned them, and left the carcasses to rot in the sun. Mitch thought that he would have to be pretty desperate to follow that line of work. Still, it was something he could do if he had to.

He recalled Tom Horn's thought about mining. If he could find the right place, that was something he could do alone. He wouldn't have to put up with the stares, the comments, and the fights that often followed. A gold mine or a silver mine in the mountains was an attractive idea, but the finding of it was the problem. Mitch wasn't at all sure that he would make much of a prospector. And in the boomtowns where the strikes were known, most of the claims were already staked, and the towns were too populous for his taste.

He gave brief consideration to bounty hunting. He had the skills for it, but the thought of killing a man he didn't even know for just a few dollars was almost as distasteful to him as hide hunting. At last he came to a decision. He would go to one of the large cattle ranches and try to get work as a ranch hand. He had worked as a cowboy before, when he was just a kid. It wasn't bad work, and the ranch hands were usually a mixed bunch of whites, Mexicans, Blacks—even some Indians and 'breeds. He should fit in all right, and he wouldn't even have to go into town at all if he didn't feel like it. He felt a little better having come to that decision.

He made his bed close to the fire and wrapped himself in his U.S. Army–issue blanket. Because of the chill in the night air, he did not undress. He left his Colt in its holster and left the belt strapped around his waist, but he pulled the six-gun around to the front so that as he slept it would be right there on top of his belly. The Winchester rifle lay across his saddle just beside him. He had almost drifted into sleep when he heard the distinct sound of approaching horses. Two, he thought. Shod. Two riders on horseback. He threw the blanket off, grabbed up his Winchester, and stepped back away from the light of the small fire. The horses came closer. Then they stopped. Mitch squinted down the trail, but he couldn't see anything out there in the dark. He waited, rifle ready.

"Hello, in the camp," a voice called out.

"Ride in slow," said Mitch.

"We ain't no road agents," the voice said as the horses' hooves again clomped on the trail. "Just a couple of weary and hungry travelers hunting a place to light for the night."

The weary travelers rode into the light. "Keep your hands where I can see them," Mitch said.

Both riders held their hands out to their sides. Both men wore heavy coats, and if they wore side arms, the coats effectively hid them. They would also prevent the men from getting at their six-guns in a hurry, if they should decide to try to pull anything like that. Mitch was aggravated. He didn't really want the company of strangers, but he couldn't send the travelers on down the road, not after dark. And the man had said that they were hungry. "All right," he said, "you can light."

The two men dismounted and started to unsaddle their horses. "We're obliged to you," said the one who had so far done all the talking. "It's a long and lonely trail, and we've been all day without a meal or even a cup of coffee."

"I've got fresh meat," Mitch said, "and coffee. Build up the fire, and I'll whip up some grub."

"That's mighty hospitable of you, friend," said the other. "My name's Homer Munson. This here's my brother, Charlie."

Mitch put his rifle down on the other side of the fire and well out of reach of the two Munsons. He didn't like their looks, and he wasn't at all happy to have any strangers for company at his camp. Even so, he couldn't turn hungry travelers away, especially at night. While Charlie poked sticks into the fire, Mitch started the coffee and the meal. It was a trail routine he was used to, and it didn't take him long. He drank another cup of coffee and rolled himself a smoke while the brothers ate.

"It don't seem right," said Homer, wiping grease from his chin with his coat sleeve, "us eating your grub and you not eating at all."

"I ate earlier," Mitch said.

"Where you headed, friend?" Charlie asked. It was the

first time he had spoken, and he talked with a mouthful of food.

"North," Mitch said.

"You don't talk much, do you?" said Homer. "Say, you never did give your name."

"No," said Mitch. "I didn't."

The brothers finished eating and finished off the coffee. Charlie shoved more sticks into the fire. "Could you spare some of them makings?" he asked. Mitch tossed them across to him, and both Munsons rolled themselves smokes. They lit them with a stick from the fire. Charlie reached across as if to hand the makings back to Mitch.

"Just toss them," Mitch said.

Charlie held them a moment before tossing them back to Mitch. "My, my," he said, "you're an untrusting sort of a soul, ain't you?" Getting no answer from Mitch, he looked at his brother. "Ain't he, Homer?"

"He does seem to be a mite edgy, Charlie," Homer said. "Reckon why. You got a reason for acting so close like, friend? Say, now that I get a good look in this firelight, you got a strong Injun look about you. You some kind of Injun, friend?"

"You ask too many questions," said Mitch.

"Hell," said Homer, "we're just trying to make friendly conversation. We couldn't help but notice how edgy you're acting, and then I got a good look at your face there. I seen that you look Injun. That's all. You got some reason for being secret like?"

"What's that got to do with my meat and coffee and tobacco?" Mitch said.

"Why, nothing, I guess," Homer said. "And you sure don't act or dress or talk like no Injun. You a half-breed, maybe?"

"That hair of his looks like Injun hair," said Charlie. "Why, I bet if someone was to take his scalp and turn it in down in Mexico, they wouldn't even ask no questions. Just pay the bounty for it. I bet they'd take it for Injun hair all right."

15

"Saddle up your horses and ride on out of here," Mitch said. "You've been fed."

"Now, that ain't friendly," Homer protested. "It's dark night."

Mitch pulled the Colt out of its holster and thumbed back the hammer. "It wouldn't be very friendly if I was to just kill you, either," he said. "Do it."

"Now, don't get careless with that thing," Homer said, rising to his feet. "Me and Charlie don't hang around where we ain't wanted. We'll get. We got us a long ways to ride anyhow. Come on, Charlie. Let's get saddled up."

The Munsons walked back to their horses and tossed the blankets on the animals' backs. Then they heaved the saddles up off the ground and swung them to the backs of the horses. Homer moved to the side of his horse to adjust the cinch, and he was hidden from Mitch's view. He reached under his coat for a revolver. Suspicious, Mitch backed away from the light, just as Homer brought his revolver up and laid his arm across his saddle. Homer fired a desperate quick shot into the darkness, missing his mark. At almost the same instant, Mitch fired, his bullet smacking into Homer's forehead. As Homer's head snapped back, Charlie ran. Mitch fired again, and Charlie yelled, staggered, and fell.

Mitch pulled the saddles off the Munsons' horses once again, then, leaving the bodies where they had fallen, he went back to bed for what was left of the night. He slept well. In the morning, he got up, put on some coffee, then searched the two bodies. He didn't find much of value, a few dollars, the guns and gun belts, and some little ammunition. Homer had carried a Smith & Wesson .44. Charlie's was an 1877 Lightning Colt, .38 caliber, with a three-and-a-half-inch barrel. He also found a .38-caliber British Bulldog in Homer's coat pocket. He dropped the little Bulldog into his own coat pocket, then took the other two revolvers over to the saddle-bags that Homer had carried. He was stuffing the side arms into the bag when he found a paper there. He pulled it out and smoothed it. In the early-morning light, he could see that it was a wanted poster, picturing the two Munsons and offering a reward of one hundred dollars for Homer and fifty dollars for Charlie—dead or alive.

"Well, I'll be damned," said Mitch to himself. "I've turned bounty hunter without even trying."

He cooked himself a breakfast and calmly ate it and drank his fill of coffee. Then he rolled himself a smoke and sat back to enjoy it. He considered that he would have to find the nearest town and hoped that he could get to it before the two bodies turned too rank to ride with. He'd have to take them along in order to collect the reward. It had been some time since Mitch had traveled this far north, and he wasn't at all sure how soon he would find a town. He didn't know what the towns would be or where or how soon he would find one. He had heard that there was silver mining activity in the foothills and mountains, though, and mining usually meant towns.

He finished his smoke, cleaned up his tin dishes, threw sand on the fire, and packed his few things. Then he saddled his horse and the two Munson horses. He loaded the bodies across their saddles, and taking the reins of the two extra horses, mounted his own and started up the trail. A hundred and fifty bucks, he thought. That's not bad for a little meat, coffee, and tobacco. Oh yeah. And two bullets.

Chapter Two

It was early evening, toward the end of a long hot day, when Mitch came to the conclusion that he would not be able to stomach the presence of the two bodies much longer. He did not want to give up the reward money, though, so he came up with an alternate plan. He stopped a little early for the night and made his camp. He threw the two bodies to the ground and unsaddled all three horses. Then he built a fire and fixed and ate his evening meal. He had a grisly task ahead of him, and he was not anxious to get into it. He rolled himself a smoke and lit it, contemplating the work he had planned for the evening. It would have to be done before dark. The sun was already close to the horizon.

Mitch tossed the butt of his smoke into the campfire and got to his feet. Pulling the big hunting knife from its sheath at his side, he walked over to the body of Homer Munson. He looked down at it for a moment, then dropped to his knees beside it. With a few deft strokes, he severed the head. Then he did the same to the body of Charlie. That was the easy part, the clean part. The rest would be really nasty. He stood up and carried the heads by their hair to a distance away from the wretched bodies and dropped them on the ground. With his knife, he scooped out a hole in the sand.

Working from the gory neck hole, Mitch cleaned out the skulls, dumping the offal into the hole he had dug. Done with the messy work, he refilled the hole, burying the mess he had made. Then he refilled the now-empty heads with sand. He carried them back over to where the headless bodies lay, took the blanket roll from Homer's rig, and untied it. Unrolling the blanket, he dumped its contents on the ground, placed the two sand-filled heads on the spread-out blanket, packed sand around them and tied the blanket up. He scooped out shallow graves for the bodies and buried them.

At last he settled down for the night. The sun was just ready to drop out of sight on the western horizon, behind the mountaintops, so he would be able to get an early start in the morning. He snugged himself into his blankets close to the small fire. The night was already growing cold. He slept well that night.

By midmorning Mitch found himself riding a mountain road, and he found that the air had not cooled since the night. He wondered if he was being stupid, for he didn't know if he would find anything up this road. Yet it seemed to be a fairly recent and well-traveled road. He thought that he would find a town up there. Then he heard the racket of a wagon coming down, and in another moment the thing appeared in the road ahead, coming at him from around a curve. He moved as far to the side of the road as he could with his three horses. The wagon was going slow, its driver not wanting to lose control on the curve. Mitch hailed the driver as the wagon drew closer to him. The scruffy-looking driver hauled back on the reins, whoaed the team, and set the brake. The man beside him sat with a grim expression on his face and held a shotgun ready.

"Howdy," the driver said. "What can I do for you?"

"Is there a town up ahead?" Mitch asked.

"You betcha," the driver said. "Town of Paxton. You can't miss it. This road runs smack through it."

"How much farther?" said Mitch.

"You ought to make it by noon," the driver said.

"Thanks," Mitch said. The driver spat tobacco juice on the road, gave Mitch a quick nod, then started the team moving again. Mitch watched the wagon for a moment, wondering what it was loaded with. Its cargo was covered by a heavy, tied-down tarp. He faced ahead again and urged his mount forward.

It was midday when Mitch saw the sign announcing that the town of Paxton was just ahead. The driver had been right. He rode on and soon was met with the sounds of a bustling, wide-open town. He could see right away that it wasn't big, but it was full and busy. The short main street, which was also the road he had been traveling, was crowded with wagons, men riding horseback, and pedestrians. There were only a few buildings. The rest of the town was made up of large canvas tents. He saw right away that two of the tents were saloons.

A boomtown, he thought. A goddamned boomtown. For a moment he thought that he might as well have gone on to Tucson with Al Sieber and Tom Horn. Boomtowns always brought the worst kind of white riffraff from all around, men who were looking for a quick way to get rich. Some were willing to work, to dig the ore out of the ground. Others came to find easier ways of getting rich: stealing from the hardworking miners, cheating them at cards, or selling to them the goods they needed at greatly inflated prices. Then there would be the whiskey sellers and the whores. And all of them, Mitch thought, would be Indian haters.

Well, hell, he told himself, I've come this far. It's too late to turn back now. He figured that he'd just collect his reward for the Munson brothers, replenish his trail supplies, maybe have a hot meal and a drink or two of whiskey, then hit the trail again. As crowded as Paxton was, it would be hard to keep out of the way of folks, but maybe, if he was lucky, he had ridden north far enough away from the Apache wars to have escaped the intense hatred that prevailed down south. Well, he'd sure as hell find out—and soon, too.

He rode on into the crowded street, maneuvering as if through a herd of cattle. He stopped his horses to allow a pedestrian to move in front of him, and to his surprise, the man looked up at him and touched the brim of his hat. "Thank you," he said.

"Is there a sheriff in this town?" Mitch asked the man.

"No, there ain't," the man said. "It's a new town. You might try the mayor's office. Just down the street on your right. His name is J. Paxton Reid."

"Paxton?" Mitch said. "That's the name of the town, ain't it?"

"That's right," the man said. "It's his town. Good luck."

The man went on about the chore of dodging wagons and other horses to get across the street, and Mitch took note of the fact that he would have to do the same thing to get to Reid. The man had said he would find the mayor's office on his right. He squinted ahead trying to find a sign, but he could not, so he started forward again, this time working his way to his right. Eventually he made it across the street, and soon after that he saw a small plank building with a sign on the false front that read, "Paxton Mining," and then, in smaller letters, "J. Paxton Reid, Mayor." He pulled up to the hitch rail, dismounted, and tied the three horses. Then he walked up to the door of the combination Paxton Mining and mayor's office and walked in.

He found himself standing in an unoccupied outer office. He wondered if it was the mining office or the mayor's office. There was a door in the back wall leading into another room. Mitch walked across the floor to it and peered in. It was a second, or inner, office, and a man was seated behind a large desk. Mitch cleared his throat, and the man looked up at him, curiosity in his expression.

"What can I do for you?" he said.

The man was maybe fifty, Mitch judged, with a slightly heavy build, a reddish face, and a receding hairline. Mitch

21

felt uncomfortable with him. "I'm looking for the mayor," he said.

"That'd be me," the man said. "I'm J. Paxton Reid. What can I do for you?"

Mitch stepped through the doorway just barely into the room and stood awkwardly. "Man down the street told me this town ain't got a sheriff," he said. "That right?"

"That's right," said Reid. "Unfortunately. Paxton's a new town, and it's grown fast. Almost too fast. It's hard to keep up with. What do you need a sheriff for? Maybe I can help."

Mitch pulled the rumpled dodger out of his pocket, walked over to Reid's desk, and laid it down. He smoothed the paper as best he could, then shoved it across the desk toward Reid. Reid looked at the poster with the Munsons pictured on it. He looked up at Mitch.

"I got them," Mitch said.

"You got them?" Reid echoed. "Where?"

"Well," Mitch said, "I got the evidence outside."

"What kind of evidence?" asked Reid.

"The hot days made them a bit rank," Mitch said. "I just brought their heads."

"You cut their heads off?" said Reid, astonished.

"It seemed like the best way," said Mitch. "You want to see them?"

"Can you bring them in here?" Reid asked.

"I can," said Mitch.

"Do it," Reid said.

Mitch walked back outside and unpacked the blanket bundle from on top of the saddle on Homer's horse. He carried it through the building to Reid's office. Reid was standing anxiously behind his desk. As Mitch came back in, Reid walked around the desk to stand in front of it. Mitch gave him a questioning look, and Reid gestured toward the floor at Mitch's feet. Mitch put down the bundle and knelt. He untied it and carefully spread the blanket. Then he brushed as much sand from the two heads as he could, enough to make them recognizable. Reid's eyes opened wide.

"Goddamn," he said. "You sure as hell did cut off their heads."

Mitch shrugged. "Like I said, it seemed like the best thing to do."

Reid turned and picked up the dodger from his desk. Then he knelt to get a better look at the ghastly trophies on his office floor. He looked again at the pictures on the dodger. "Yeah," he said. "Uh-huh. This one here's Homer, all right, and this here is Charlie. Sure enough. You got them, all right, and you should have a hundred and fifty dollars coming to you for it. No question about it." He stood up and went back around to his chair to sit. "Tell me about it," he said.

"Ain't much to tell," Mitch said. "I was camped. They came in. They tried to get the drop on me, and I killed them. Then I found this handbill in their saddlebags. Figured I might as well go ahead and collect on them."

"You're not a bounty hunter, then?" Reid asked.

"No, I ain't," said Mitch. "Not by choice. They just happened on me. That's all."

"I see," said Reid. "I see." He was obviously pondering something. "What is your trade," he said, "if I may ask?"

"Right now I guess I ain't got one," Mitch said. "I was a scout for the army, but General Miles cut us all loose."

"You worked for Crook?" Reid asked.

"That's right," said Mitch.

"With Al Sieber and Tom Horn? Chasing Geronimo?"

"That was our job."

"Well, well," Reid mused. "A real manhunter. I got a man I want hunted down. You want the job?"

"What about my money for these two?" Mitch asked.

"I'll have to telegraph the sheriff over at the county seat," said Reid. "It'll take a little while, but I expect we'll get it for you. What about the job?"

"I don't know," Mitch said. "All I come in here for was to get my money."

"That's only a hundred and fifty," said Reid. "I'll pay you five hundred if you run down my man."

"Why me?" Mitch asked. "You've got a town full of

men here, and five hundred's a lot of money. You could just yell out the front door for a man.''

"There's no real manhunters out there," said Reid, "and besides, in a boomtown like Paxton, money's the cheapest thing we got. No miner's going to risk his neck for five hundred when he could dig out several thousand in the time it would take him to track a man down. No gambler's going to do it either. He could fleece a dozen miners in the same time. What do you say? You have to hang around awhile to wait for your hundred and fifty anyhow."

"When you wire that sheriff," said Mitch, "ask him about their horses and guns, too. I've got them."

"All right," Reid said. "I will. What's your name, anyhow?"

"Mitch Frye."

"Mitch Frye," Reid repeated. "You Indian?"

"My father was an Apache," Mitch said. "I never knew him. My mother was white."

Reid wrote himself a note. "Well, Mitch," he said, "what do you say? You want to lay around and get drunk while you wait for a hundred and fifty, or you want to go for an additional five hundred to put with it?"

Chapter Three

Mitch rode out early the following morning. He'd had a bath and a shave, and he'd spent the night in a bed under a roof following a good hot meal, all on credit established for him by J. Paxton Reid. From the little he had seen of Paxton, the man in the street had been right. It was Reid's town. He felt a little like Reid had taken advantage of him, but then he thought it wasn't really all that much. And after all, he stood to ride out of Paxton in a few days with over six hundred dollars instead of just one hundred fifty. An extra five hundred just for tracking down one man.

The man's name was Duncklee, according to Reid, and he was about six foot three, lanky, with shaggy hair and beard. He had the look of a miner, but he was actually a fellow with an engineering degree from somewhere back east. He had been in charge of mining operations for Reid up until just the night before Mitch had ridden into town. That morning, payday at the mine, an office worker out at the mine was found dead in the office with his head bashed in by a shovel. The safe was standing open and empty. Duncklee had disappeared with one saddle horse, one packhorse, and one hundred thousand of J. Paxton Reid's dollars. Reid wanted it all back, the money, the horses, and Duncklee. It would be all right, he had told Mitch, if Mitch brought only part of him back, the way he had done with the Munsons.

There was only one way he could have gone, Reid had said. If Mitch followed the road on out of Paxton and continued up the mountain, it would lead him to the mines. There it stopped. Duncklee was not up there. The road Mitch had come to town on was the only road out of Paxton and down the mountain. There was no way a man with two horses could get off the road and into the mountains. He had to go down the road. Once down, of course, he could go any direction.

Mitch calculated all the possibilities and weighed them one against the other. He eliminated the possibility of Duncklee's heading south. Things were still pretty hot down in that direction, with the Geronimo campaign in full force. Of course, a desperate man might try for a ride through to Tucson, but it seemed more likely that a man with a hundred thousand on him would want to play it safe—as safe as possible in this country. Besides, Mitch thought that if Duncklee had gone south, it was likely he would have seen him along the way.

It wouldn't make sense for a man, especially one inexperienced in this country, to take off across the wide-open spaces. He wouldn't know where to find water, and he would most likely lose his bearings and wander in circles until he died of hunger or thirst or exhaustion or the heat or the night cold or something. Mitch thought that Duncklee would keep to the road and head for the nearest civilization. From there he would probably sell the horses and buy a stage ticket for the next coach headed east. He was an easterner with a hundred thousand in cash. He'd be headed home.

No one knew just what time the man at the mine office had been killed, so Mitch did not know how much of a head start Duncklee had on him. He knew that he'd had all of yesterday and all of last night. How much of the night before he had used was unknown. If he had killed the man in the late evening or early night, he would have had all that night, so it was possible that Duncklee had as much as twenty-eight or thirty hours on him. But he couldn't have been riding all that time. He had to rest the horses, and he had to have some sleep himself.

Mitch could recall two spots along the road down the mountain where it was wide enough to stop and camp. He didn't think the man would have done that, though. Having just killed a man and stolen all that money, he most likely would have wanted to get as much distance between himself and Paxton as he could before he stopped to rest. He figured that Duncklee would have ridden all night to get down the mountain, then stopped for a rest in the morning. When he came to the first of the two spots, he stopped and dismounted to examine the ground. He found no evidence of a recent camp there. That was all right. He hadn't expected to find anything there.

He was about to mount up and resume his ride when he heard the sounds of a wagon coming up the road. He waited. In another moment the wagon hove into view. Two men were on the seat. The wagon was loaded full. Mitch hailed it. The driver pulled to a halt.

"Howdy, stranger," he called out. The other man nodded.

"What you hauling there?" Mitch asked.

"Supplies for Paxton," the driver answered.

"As busy as that little town is," Mitch said, "I bet they keep you running back and forth pretty regular."

"That's right," the driver said. "You riding up or down?"

"I'm going down," Mitch said. "I'm looking for a man name of Duncklee."

"From up at the mine?" the driver said. "I know him."

"Have you seen him?"

"Ain't seen hide nor hair of him," the driver answered. "Not since my last trip up. I seen him then. He was drunk."

"Falling-down drunk," said the other man, and then both men on the wagon seat broke into raucous laughter, apparently recalling some episode involving Duncklee's drunkenness. Their laughter subsided, and Mitch climbed back into the saddle.

"What you hunting old Duncklee for?" the driver asked.

"He disappeared," said Mitch. "Reid's paying me to find him."

"Disappeared?" the driver said. "Well, I be damned."

"Reckon where he went to?" said the other man.

"It's my job to find that out," said Mitch. He touched the brim of his hat and urged his horse forward. "Obliged to you."

Later he stopped to check the other possible camp site, but he found no evidence there that Duncklee had stopped. He passed several travelers on the road, all on their way to Paxton for various reasons. None of them had seen anyone fitting the description of Duncklee. Mitch decided that he had been right in his judgment that Duncklee had ridden all night to get down the mountain. But then, if none of the travelers had seen him, where did he go? Did he ride south or leave the road to ride across open country? Either way, Mitch figured, the man was not only a thief and a murderer but a fool as well.

It was dusk by the time Mitch reached the bottom of the mountain road. He continued on, looking for a likely spot to camp for the night. The road turned and headed northeast, running alongside a clear, fast-moving river. It wasn't long before Mitch came to a place beside the river that would serve. He turned his horse off the road, and then he saw the signs of a recent camp. Even in the dimming light, he could tell that a man with two horses had camped there. Duncklee. Almost for sure. From the ashes and the horse turds, he figured that the fugitive was still at least a day's ride ahead of him. He decided that he'd wait for morning light to see if he could find tracks that would tell him which way Duncklee had gone from here. He built a small fire, cooked himself a meal, brewed some coffee, ate, drank his fill, and smoked a cigarette. Then he turned in for the night.

*　　*　　*

The morning light showed Mitch that Duncklee had gone back to the road and headed north. It didn't make sense that none of the travelers had seen the man, unless they had passed by his camp without noticing it. If that had been the case, then Duncklee had slept for quite a spell, and he might not be as far ahead as Mitch had thought before. He followed the tracks back to the well-traveled road and soon they were lost in a multitude of other evidence. Mitch rode slowly, watching the edge of the road for any signs that might indicate that Duncklee had left the road again. It wasn't long before he found them. The man had headed almost due east across open country. Mitch followed.

The sun was high in the sky, and the day was getting hot when Mitch saw that Duncklee had turned north again. The man wasn't as big a fool as he had thought. He was headed for civilization and a stage line, but he was smart enough to get off the road so that he wouldn't be seen. Obviously his plan was to ride parallel to the road, probably for most of the way to the next town. Mitch stayed on the trail. He hurried his horse along for a while, then slowed him to a walk again. He didn't want to wear down his mount, but he did hope to catch up to Duncklee while they were still out in the open and alone.

Suddenly and surprisingly, the landscape broke up into a series of rolling hills, dry washes, and gullies. The trail was harder to follow, so Mitch moved slowly, watching the ground. A shot rang out and a bullet whizzed close by Mitch's head. He flung himself from the saddle and rolled quickly to a low spot off to his left to seek shelter. He was caught by surprise. Could he be that close to Duncklee? He hadn't thought so. But who else would be shooting at him, and why?

Mitch cursed himself for having been caught off guard. His rifle was still on his horse. He hadn't had time to grab it when he jumped for cover. Going for it now would expose him to another shot. His revolver was next to useless in this situation. He tried to study the terrain ahead without raising his head up too much. He couldn't think of a thing to do

29

except try to inch his way around to better cover, then hope that he'd be able to sneak ahead and get close to Duncklee, if that's who was shooting at him. Then he heard the sound of pounding hooves.

The man must have figured that he had hit Mitch and was riding away. At least he must have thought, having unhorsed his pursuer, he could escape. But it could be a trick. Duncklee had two horses. It sounded to Mitch like only one horse was running. He got halfway up and ran in a crouch to his horse. No shot was fired. He grabbed his Winchester and, staying in a crouch, ran to the top of a nearby rise. He saw the man riding hard, heading north. The distance was too great for a sure rifle shot, so Mitch decided not to even try it from there. He ran back to his horse, mounted up, and started his pursuit.

He rode past a downed horse. That was what had slowed the man. His quick glimpse as he hurried by told him that the saddle horse had gone lame. Desperate, Duncklee had dumped the pack from the other horse and saddled it to ride. Topping another rise, Mitch could see that he had closed the distance between him and his quarry. He stopped and dismounted. Quieting his horse, he laid the rifle across the saddle and sighted it in on the back of the fleeing Duncklee. He considered a warning shot, but discarded that thought. If Duncklee ignored the warning, Mitch might not have time for a second shot. And after all, the man was a murderer and a thief. Mitch pulled the trigger.

An instant later, the rider in the distance flung his arms up over his head, then flipped backward out of the saddle. The riderless horse ran on. Mitch mounted up and rode slowly toward where the man lay still in the dirt. He chambered another shell in case Duncklee was still alive and playing possum, but he didn't really think that would be the case. Holding the rifle ready, he rode up close to the body. He could see that his bullet had hit its mark, right between the shoulder blades. He could also see that the man had been a tall and lanky man.

Mitch dismounted, still carefully, then nudged the body

with his boot. It was still. He shoved harder and turned it over. The face was grim in death. It was also half covered with a shaggy beard. The hair on the head was long and shaggy. The man certainly fit the description of Duncklee given to Mitch by Reid, and he had been traveling with a packhorse. Then there was the matter of the stolen money. Satisfied that he had killed Duncklee, Mitch went after the loose horse.

It had run on for a while and then slowed. Mitch saw it not too far ahead, trotting aimlessly in circles. He would have to approach the skittish beast easy so as not to startle it. He rode slowly. The horse ahead at last stopped trotting and milled around looking for something to nibble on. Mitch rode slowly toward it. When he got close enough, he talked softly. The horse raised its head, nickered, and trotted a short distance away. Mitch talked to it some more and rode slowly toward it. This time he was able to get close enough to reach the dangling reins. He turned around and rode back to the body, leading the horse.

He checked the saddlebags first, and there he found the money. Mitch felt some relief, for now he was sure that he had killed the right man. He transferred the cash to the saddlebags on his own horse, then set about the ghastly task of removing and packing Duncklee's head, just as he had done with the two Munsons. That bloody chore done, he unsaddled the packhorse and put the pack back on its back. The extra saddle and the wrapped-up, sand-packed head were added to the pack. Mitch scooped out a shallow grave and buried the headless corpse.

Chapter Four

Mitch walked into Reid's office unannounced and without a knock. As Reid's head snapped up from the paperwork he was engaged in, Mitch dropped the bundle onto the office floor. Without a word, he knelt and unwrapped the ghastly head. "Is this your man?" he asked.

"That's Duncklee," Reid said. "What about the—"

Mitch tossed his saddlebags onto Reid's desk. "In there," he said.

Reid dug into the bags for his money. He hauled it out greedily and counted it before saying another word or looking up at Mitch again. Then, with a look of some relief, he said, "It's all there."

"I brought back one horse," said Mitch. "The other one's dead. The horse and pack—everything he had with him—is all outside."

Reid looked up with a smile on his face. Then he counted out five hundred dollars and handed it across the desk to Mitch. "That's what I promised you," he said. "And I got authorization to pay the reward for the Munsons.'' He counted another hundred and fifty and handed that to Mitch. ''The sheriff wired that you can keep the rest of the Munsons' stuff,'' he added. ''Horses, guns, whatever. As far as I'm concerned, you can keep what you brought back of Duncklee's, too. You can most likely sell the horses down at the end of the road to old Sam Neely, if you don't want to keep them.''

''Thanks,'' said Mitch. ''I'll be on my way.''

''Wait a minute,'' Reid said. ''Let me buy you a drink.'' He opened a desk drawer and brought out a bottle and two glasses. ''There's a matter of a little paperwork before you leave anyhow. Have a chair.''

Mitch saw a straight wooden chair against the wall. He pulled it up to the desk and took the glass Reid offered him. Then Reid passed over a sheet of paper and a pencil. Mitch picked it up and read it. It was a receipt for the hundred and fifty dollars for the Munsons. Mitch signed it. Reid passed over a second sheet. It was a statement swearing that Mitch had killed and brought in the heads of the Munsons for reward. He signed that one, too. Reid passed a third sheet over, but it was blank. Mitch gave him a look.

''What's this for?'' he asked.

''I need a statement for the records,'' said Reid. ''Just write that you tracked down Duncklee and killed him. That's all.''

Mitch wrote, ''I, Mitch Frye, tracked down a man named Duncklee and killed him. I brought in his head for pay.'' He signed the paper and shoved it back toward Reid. Then he turned up his glass and finished the whiskey. Reid quickly offered a second drink.

''No, thanks,'' said Mitch. ''I reckon I'll just be on my way.''

''Don't be in such a hurry,'' Reid said. ''I've got a little proposition for you. I just put six hundred and fifty dollars in your hands. The least you can do is listen to me.''

Mitch settled back in the chair. ''All right,'' he said.

Reid poured the glass full again. "Paxton needs a sheriff," he said. "I'm offering you the job."

"What for?" said Mitch. "You don't even know me."

"I know all I need to know," Reid answered. "You told me you worked for General Crook with Al Sieber and Tom Horn. I checked up on it while you were gone and got it confirmed. You were with them for four years. That's a hell of a good recommendation. You brought in the heads of those Munsons, and then I gave you another job. You did it. You tracked down Duncklee and brought me his head. What's more, you brought my money back. Some men would have just kept riding with that much cash on them."

"I'm no thief," Mitch said.

"That's what I mean," Reid said. "You've got experience, you're a good manhunter and good in a fight, and you're honest. That's all I need to know. What do you say?"

"I never thought about being no lawman," said Mitch.

"Steady pay," said Reid. "I'll find you a place to live."

"Thanks," said Mitch, "but I ain't interested. I think I'll just ride on."

"I'll pay you a hundred dollars a month plus room and board," Reid said.

"No," Mitch said. He put the glass on the desk. It was still almost full of whiskey. "I appreciate the offer, but I ain't no lawman. I'll be leaving now."

Mitch was halfway across the room when Reid stopped him with a sharp tone of voice. "Mitch," he said. Mitch looked back over his shoulder and saw Reid holding up the last sheet of paper he had written on. Reid was grinning. "This is a confession," he said.

"What?"

"It's in your own handwriting and it's signed," Reid said. "It says that you killed Duncklee and cut off his head. That's murder. And cutting off your victim's head will make it worse in the eyes of a white jury, Mitch."

"You sent me after that man," Mitch said. "You paid me for the job. He was a killer and a thief."

"There was never any complaint filed against him," Reid

said. "He wasn't wanted. You can't prove that it was any-thing but murder."

"Just what are you getting at?" Mitch asked, walking back toward Reid.

"Either you accept my offer," Reid said, "or I wire the sheriff again. You'll be a wanted man, hunted everywhere you go. You'll be hounded until you're shot and killed or captured and hanged."

"You son of a bitch," said Mitch.

"That may be," Reid said. "I have a contract here for the job. You want to sign it?"

That night Mitch knocked two drunks on their heads to calm them down. Paxton had no jail in which to throw them, so that would have to do. He also broke up a fistfight in one of the tent saloons. Then, things beginning to quiet down for the night, he went to the room Reid had found for him. It was in a small building, very much like the one Reid's of-fices were in. The front room, Reid had said, would serve as the sheriff's office. The back room was Mitch's living space. The room had been hastily furnished with a cot, a small table, and a water bowl. Mitch had tossed his blanket roll in there. The office was still bare.

Mitch had the most restless night he had suffered in quite some time. His sleep was troubled by both his situation and his surroundings. He was furious with Reid for having tricked him into accepting the sheriff's job. He was angry at himself for having so easily fallen into the slick bastard's trap. He was totally uncomfortable with the new job, and he could hardly stand the rowdy town he was now stuck in. There was someone making noise somewhere all through the night.

Early the next morning, Reid came into the sheriff's office. Mitch had just finished dressing and was strapping on his Colt. "Morning, Sheriff," Reid said with a wide grin on his face. Mitch felt like wiping the grin off the man's face, but he knew that would only bring him more trouble than he wanted in his young life. He glanced at Reid and said nothing. "You did a good job last night," Reid said.

"This town needs a jail," Mitch said.

"You're right about that," Reid agreed. "And we'll build you one right away. That's at the top of the list. Right now, let's go get you some breakfast. I promised you room and board, didn't I? We'll see about the board right now."

Reid led the way down the street to a large tent with a sign out front that read, "Eat Here." They went inside and found themselves two seats at a long table.

The place was already busy. Reid waved a hand at a young woman who was bustling from one table to another, carrying plates of food to customers or taking away dirty dishes. When she noticed Reid waving, she hurried over, and Mitch recalled again the statement of the man in the street: *"It's his town."*

"Good morning, Pax," the woman said with a sudden pleasant smile on her face. "What can I do for you?"

"We'll have us some ham and eggs," Reid said, "but first I want you to meet our new sheriff. This is Mitch Frye. Mitch, this lady is Ellie West. She owns this establishment. Now Ellie, as sheriff, Mitch is paid a salary and room and board. I want you to give him anything he wants anytime he comes in here. Just keep a tab and turn it in at the mayor's office once a week."

"All right, Pax," Ellie said. "You want coffee?"

"Two coffees," Reid said, and Mitch nodded.

The breakfast was not bad, Mitch thought, and at least he knew where he could get regular meals. When they were done, Reid walked with him back to Mitch's new office, and they stepped inside the bare room.

"I'll get you some furniture over here later today," Reid said, "and I'll get some men to work on a jailhouse right away. Anything else you need right now?"

"If I'm supposed to be enforcing the laws," Mitch said, "I need to know what they are. You got a law book or something?"

"Paxton's still too new for that," Reid said. "We'll get

around to electing a town council one of these days and formalizing the laws. For right now just use your good sense. No brawling or shooting off guns in town. No thieving or killing. No rape. You know. Just use your head."

Reid went on about his business, and Mitch decided to look the town over. He went out the front door of his office and started to walk down the street toward the mine end of the road. He passed by a small tent with a sign in front that read, "Claims Office," a large plank building that was called a general store and advertised "everything you need at the best prices available," a tent saloon already serving drinks, a whorehouse in a tent, and finally he came to Sam Neely's combination blacksmith shop and stable. A sweaty man was busy bending over an anvil and pounding a horseshoe with a hammer. Mitch stood there waiting. At last the man straightened up and looked in his direction.

"Can I help you, mister?" he said.

"My name's Mitch Frye," Mitch said. "I'm the new sheriff."

"Sheriff?" said the other. "First I've heard of it."

"I said I was new," said Mitch. "Are you Neely?"

"That's right," said the sweaty blacksmith.

"Mr. Reid told me that I might be able to sell you some horses," Mitch said.

"Could be," said Neely. "How many you got?"

"Three to sell," said Mitch. "One to board."

"Bring them around and let me look at them," said Neely.

"Got three extra saddles, too," Mitch said.

"Bring them around."

Mitch looked up the side of the mountain, and he could see the large Paxton mine up above, dominating the town. "Is that the only mine in town?" he asked.

"The Paxton?" said Neely. "It's the biggest. By far. There's other small ones around here and there, though. Lot of single miners working their own claims, too."

"Well," Mitch said, "I'll bring those horses around a little later."

He crossed the street and started walking back the other

way. He figured that he might as well start getting familiar with the town he was supposed to ride herd on. He spent the rest of that morning walking the one street of Paxton, stopping here and there to introduce himself and receiving a few hard looks from people along the way. Toward noon he went back to the "Eat Here" tent and had himself a lunch. Ellie wrote it down on the tab, and Mitch thanked her kindly and walked back to his office. There were three straight chairs in the front room. He checked the back room and found a chair in there. He rolled himself a smoke and stretched out on the cot to enjoy it.

Soon he heard some clatter coming from the front room, and got up to go see what was causing it. Two men were lugging a large wooden desk into the room. "Where do you want it?" one of them asked when he saw Mitch. Mitch pointed toward the back wall.

"Over there," he said. He figured that he could sit behind the desk and face the front door. The men carried the desk into place, and Mitch picked up one of the chairs and moved it behind the desk. "Thanks," he said. The two men left, and Mitch sat down behind his new desk. He opened the drawers one at a time and found them all empty except the wide one in the middle. In there was a stack of blank sheets of paper and a few pencils. Mitch harrumphed and shut the drawer. He thought a minute, then reopened it and took out a sheet of paper and a pencil. He started to make a list.

    gun cabinet
    stove
    coffeepot
    coffee
    water bucket

A question intruded on the list: "Where do I draw water?"

Bored already with the chore, he got up and left the office. He took the three horses and saddles down to Sam Neely and sold them for a nice sum. Leaving his own horse and

saddle to board, he went back to his office. There he unpacked the things left behind by the Munsons and by Duncklee. He folded the blankets and tossed them in a corner of
the room. He might need them later for the jail, he thought,
if Reid ever got around to having one built. The extra handguns went into a desk drawer, and he leaned the extra rifles
in a corner of the room. Boxes of shells also went into a
desk drawer. The rest of the stuff was trash, as far as he was
concerned. He gathered it up and went through his living
quarters to the back door. Opening the door, he pitched it
out. He'd figure out what to do with it later. Burn it, maybe.

He went back to his desk and resumed his seat. Picking
up the pencil, he added to the list "trash?" Then he thought
of another question, and he wrote it down. "Do I have a
budget for this office?" He looked at his list for a moment,
then picked it up and took it with him out of the office. He
walked down the street to the office of the mayor and barged
in. He stalked all the way through the front office and was
already talking as he strode across the threshold into the private office of J. Paxton Reid.

"If you're going to force me to be sheriff of this dog-ass
town—"

He stopped in midsentence, for sitting there in a chair beside Reid's desk was a lovely young lady. Mitch whipped
the hat off his head and held it in both hands in front of his
chest.

"I beg your pardon, ma'am," he said. "I didn't expect—
Well, please forgive me for stomping in like that, and for
my language." He glanced at Reid. "I'll come back later,"
he said.

"Come on in, Mitch," Reid said. "It's all right. She's
heard it all anyhow. This is my daughter, Jewel. Jewel, this
is our new sheriff, Mitch Frye."

Jewel smiled and gave Mitch a look that told him he was
forgiven for his rude entrance. "How do you do, Mr. Frye,"
she said.

"Oh, just fine, ma'am," he said. "It's a real pleasure to
meet you, I'm sure."

"Now, you were saying something when you came in," Reid said.

"It can wait," Mitch said. "I didn't intend to interrupt nothing."

"We're just visiting," said Jewel. "I don't mind."

"What is it, Mitch?" Reid said.

Mitch walked on over to the desk and held the paper out to Reid. "I made up this here list," he said. "Some of it is stuff I need, and then there's a couple of questions there, too."

Reid took the list and gave it a quick glance. "I'll look this over and get back to you," he said. "Is there anything else?"

"No," said Mitch. "No, there ain't. Well, I'll be seeing you."

As he stepped out into the street again, Mitch sucked in a deep breath. Damn, he said to himself, who'd have ever thought that the sleazy son of bitch would be father to something like that? He had embarrassed himself, and he didn't like that, especially not in front of Reid. Well, damn it, he told himself, I'm stuck here, and I'll just have to make the best of it. He decided that he'd have to calm down and learn to roll with the punches.

Chapter Five

As the days passed by slowly, Mitch almost grew used to the nearly constant noise of the busy little town of Paxton. He developed a routine for his new job. He told himself that things could be worse. He had money, more money than he'd ever had in his life, and he just seemed to keep piling it up, for he had very little on which to spend it. He bought himself some new clothes, and he had an occasional drink of good whiskey. Now and then he got into a poker game. Sometimes he won and sometimes he lost. But neither the whiskey nor the poker became an addiction, and he didn't spend or lose much money there. His meals were all paid for by the town of Paxton, as was his lodging. He didn't meet anyone he would actually call friend, but he did make some few acquaintances he could sit and visit with for at least a few minutes before he tired of the conversation.

But his deep resentment toward J. Paxton Reid continued. There were no two ways about it. The man was holding him prisoner. He was a well-treated prisoner, true enough, but a prisoner nonetheless. As long as Reid held that paper that Mitch had written, Mitch was not free, and that one fact ate at him almost constantly. Now and then he considered slipping off in the middle of the night, calling Reid's bluff. But he wondered—would the bastard actually have him charged with the murder of Duncklee? Mitch couldn't be sure, but sometimes he thought that the life of a fugitive would be preferable to this comfortable prison he was in.

He was walking down the street after a lunch of beef stew at Ellie West's establishment when he turned into Reid's office. He wasn't sure why. He wanted to complain to Reid again about the situation he was in, but he knew that it would do no good. Even so, he went in. Stepping into the back office, he saw that Reid was not in. He walked back through the front office and moved to the front door. Opening the door, he looked out on the busy street. He saw no sign of Reid and started to leave again, but he hesitated. He thought for a moment, then stepped back inside and closed the door.

He hurried into Reid's office and moved around behind the big desk. He jerked open one drawer and then another, rifling through the papers he found there. He had looked in the last desk drawer without finding the paper he was looking for. He got up and moved to a cabinet on the wall to his right and opened it up. There were more papers there, and he started thumbing through them. He was deeply involved in his search when the voice of Reid startled him. "Looking for this?" Reid said. Mitch jerked around to see Reid standing in the doorway holding up a folded piece of paper. "I keep it on me all the time," Reid added.

"I could take it away from you," Mitch said.

"You could," Reid agreed. "I have no doubt of that. But if you attack me, take it away from me, and leave me alive, I'll swear out a complaint on you for assault. If you kill me and leave town, they'll be looking for you for my murder."

"It might be worth it," Mitch said, his hand moving to the Colt at his side.

"No, it wouldn't," said Reid. "Forget it. You can't win, Mitch. I've got you."

"For now," said Mitch, his hand relaxing and falling back to his side. "Nothing lasts forever."

"Mitch," said Reid, "sit down and have a drink with me."

"It's too early," Mitch said, "and I'm particular who I drink with."

"All right. Suit yourself," Reid said as he moved around behind his desk to sit in the big stuffed chair. "But tell me. What's wrong with your setup here? I'm paying you well. You got a place to live, three meals a day. I've given you everything you asked for. They're working on the new jail right now. What do you want from me?"

"I don't want a damn thing from you," said Mitch. "And that includes your job."

"Well, you've got the job," Reid said with finality. "You might as well get that set in your head. Is there anything else?"

"Not a goddamn thing," Mitch said, and he turned and walked out the door. He felt footloose. There was really nothing to do. Most days, he walked the streets and found everything relatively calm all day long. Besides the rest, the job was simply boring. Mitch found most of his hours idle. He was piling up unearned money. He longed to be out riding the trail, tracking . . . anyone. Then he heard a gunshot. He turned to look in the direction from which the sound had come, and then there was another. He moved toward the Golden Monkey, a tent saloon across the street and up the mountain about a hundred yards.

Fighting his way across the heavy street traffic, Mitch unholstered his Colt. He stopped at the front door of the Golden Monkey. There was another shot. He eased himself around the gathered tent flap door and at first thought he was looking into an empty saloon. Then he saw the big man at the bar, and next he saw men under the tables. The man at the bar fired another shot into the canvas roof overhead. That was four shots. He had at best two more. Mitch watched as the big man turned back to the bar and reached for a glass. The glass was empty, and the big man threw it across the room.

He picked up a bottle, looked at it, and threw it after the glass.

"Barkeep," he shouted. There was no immediate response, so he roared again. "Give me another bottle or I'll come around there behind that bar with you."

An arm came up from behind the bar to place a bottle there. The arm vanished again, and the big man grabbed the bottle by its neck. As he tipped the bottle up for a long drink, Mitch moved quietly into the big room. He started moving slowly and cautiously toward the bar, circling behind the big man. The big man banged the bottle down on the bar with his left hand and raised his revolver up again in his right. He fired again. Mitch calculated that if the gun had been loaded with only five bullets, it was now empty. But it might have been loaded with six. Mitch stood still.

"You're under arrest," he said in a loud voice, and the big man whirled and raised his revolver. Mitch ducked as a last shot rang out. That's it, he said to himself as he straightened up and moved in quickly on the big man. The big man tried to fire again but realized that his revolver was empty. He threw it at Mitch, but his aim was wide. Mitch was closing in, and the big man grabbed up a chair. Mitch dodged as the chair whistled by his head. The big man had swung so hard that he spun himself around. Mitch, now standing behind the man, raised his Colt up high and brought the barrel down hard on the man's head. The man stood stunned for a moment, then pitched forward to fall on his face on the hard wood floor. The bartender stood up slowly to peek over the edge of the bar at the prone figure there.

"Do you know him?" Mitch asked.

"That's Big Bob," the bartender said. "I think his name's McNamara, but they always just call him Big Bob. He's part owner of a mine uphill from here. Other side of the Paxton mine. Him and George Orr. He's been in here since last night. He gets this way about once a month."

"He ever hurt anyone when he was like this?" Mitch asked.

"Broke Mike Carter's arm last month," the bartender said.

"Get a couple of men to drag him over to my office," Mitch said. He left the saloon and went back to his sheriff's office. He paused in the office just long enough to pick up a length of chain and a padlock. Then he went out the back door, where, a few feet away, men were busy building the new jail. Mitch had the workers hold up a log they were about to set in place while he wrapped the chain around it a couple of times. He was ready by the time two men from the saloon dragged the still-unconscious Big Bob over. Mitch wrapped the end of the chain around Big Bob's ankle and slipped the lock through two links, securing Big Bob to the as-yet-unfinished jail.

"That'll hold him," he said.

It was not more than an hour and a half later that Reid came into the sheriff's office with another man, a hard rock miner by his looks. Mitch was sitting at his desk writing a report on his arrest of Big Bob. He looked up.

"Mitch," said Reid, "this is Manny Gordon. He just reported a killing to me. Manny, tell it to Mitch here. He's the sheriff. Tell him just what you told me."

"Well," said Manny, "just like I said. I was coming into town from my place, and I thought I'd stop by and have a shot of coffee with old George. George Orr, that is. George and Big Bob's my neighbors. I hollered around, and no one answered me. I seen that Big Bob's horse was gone, but George's old mule was there, so I looked inside the shack, and that's when I seen him. George was laying there on the floor dead."

"You said a murder," Mitch said to Reid.

"Tell him," Reid said.

"Well, Sheriff," Manny said, "first I just seen that he was just laying there, so I went on in to see if he was maybe alive and I could help him some way, but when I stepped in closer I seen that his head was bashed in. Looked like someone hit him with a hammer or something. I hurried out of there then. Come right in here and straight to the mayor's office."

"Sound like a murder to you?" Reid asked Mitch.

"Sounds like," said Mitch. He thought about the bashed-in head of the man Duncklee had been accused of killing, and he thought about George Orr's drunken and violent partner chained to the wall of the unfinished jail out back. "Manny," he said, "can you show me the way out there?"

Chapter Six

Mitch looked carefully around the miners' shack and along the trail leading up to it. He found tracks, but they could have been the tracks of the two partners or of Manny. He was able to determine those of Manny right away. He called himself stupid for not having checked the boots of Big Bob before leaving the office. However, he thought that the largest prints probably belonged to his prisoner. That meant nothing regarding the murder, of course, for Big Bob would have been all over this place. In a moment he would check the feet of the corpse inside the shack. He should be able to eliminate the prints of Big Bob, George Orr, and Manny. That done, he would study what prints remained unidentified.

He turned to Manny and said, "Follow me, Manny. Stay right behind me. I don't want these prints messed up any more than they have been already."

"I'll step right in your footprints," Manny said.

Mitch led the way into the shack, and Manny followed. The light was dim inside the small, cluttered shack, but not too dim to see. The place had the look that Mitch expected for a mining shack occupied by two bachelor partners. Right away he saw the legs of the corpse, but he didn't move right away. He stood still and looked around. He saw no sign of a struggle. He figured that Orr must have known his attacker well enough to have let him in the shack and even to have turned his back on the man. He stepped on in and knelt beside the body.

Just as Manny had said, the skull had been bashed in from behind. Just like, he couldn't help thinking, the body of the man at the Paxton mine, the man Duncklee had been accused of killing. But this killing had been done too recently for Duncklee to have done it. Perhaps Duncklee had not been guilty after all, and Mitch had killed the man and decapitated his body. It had been Reid who had accused Duncklee, Reid who had sent Mitch out to get the man. He wondered if Reid had perhaps been responsible for the first murder as well as for this one. If so, that would make Reid responsible for three deaths.

He tried to shake that thought out of his mind. It was too soon to be jumping to conclusions. There was also Orr's drunken partner to consider. Big Bob was obviously prone to violence, and he had been wildly drunk just the night before. He could have started at the shack, killed his partner, then gone to town to continue his rampage. He decided that he'd learned all he could from the body, and it hadn't been any more than what Manny had already told him. Orr had been hit hard from behind. Manny had said by something like a hammer. Reid had said that the other man had been killed by a blow from a shovel.

"Manny," Mitch said, "help me load him up."

They tied the body onto the back of the mule outside that had belonged to Orr, and Mitch told Manny to take it to town. There was nothing more to learn from Manny. Mitch had needed him mainly to lead the way to the mine. As Manny headed back toward Paxton with his grim cargo, Mitch went back inside the shack. He found nothing resembling a murder weapon. He did find a shovel and a hammer, but they had no trace of blood on them, and they were dusty, so no one had wiped them clean recently.

He was interested in the fact that he found no whiskey, not even empty bottles. Apparently Big Bob did all his drinking in town. That meant that if Bob had killed Orr, he had been sober at the time. Then he had gone into town to get drunk. Poking around some more, Mitch overturned a bucket he found underneath one of the beds. He found two bags of gold nuggets there.

If someone had killed Orr to rob him, the killer had failed to find the gold. However, the gold was a motive for Big Bob. If the partners had struck gold, Bob could have killed Orr to keep from having to share their gains. But then, why not take the gold and get out? Why leave it in the shack and go to town to get drunk? He put the gold back where he had found it, stood up, and walked outside. The light was bright, causing him to squint for a moment. He studied the tracks again, setting them in his mind. There were four recent sets: Orr's, Manny's, the large prints that were likely Big Bob's, and an unidentified set.

And there were the hoofprints. Mitch identified those of Orr's mule easily. Manny had walked. There were the prints of two horses. One horse must have belonged to Big Bob. The other might belong to the killer. At last he decided that he had learned all he could from the scene of the crime. He mounted up and rode back to town. As he approached his office, Reid stepped out into the street and hailed him. Mitch hauled back on the reins to stop his horse. "What did you find out there?" Reid asked him.

"Just what Manny told us I'd find," said Mitch.

"What are you going to do about it?" Reid demanded.

"I'm going to talk to Big Bob first," said Mitch.

"And then?"

"I don't know," Mitch said. "You tell me."

He urged his mount forward, brushing past Reid, and went on to his office. He dismounted and slapped the reins around the hitching rail. Then he walked through the office and out the back to the new jail. Big Bob was rolling in the dirt and moaning. Mitch gave him a kick to get his attention. Bob groaned and looked up. "Who are you?" he said.

"I'm the sheriff," said Mitch.

"Well, let me out of here," Bob said. "Someone put this damn chain around me."

"You're in jail," Mitch said.

"In jail? This ain't no jail," Bob complained. "I'm chained to a goddamned log."

"That's the best we can do," said Mitch. "Do you know why you've been arrested?"

"I don't remember nothing," said Bob. "I was just having a little fun. That's all. My head hurts."

"I bent my gun barrel over it," said Mitch. "You were shooting up the Golden Monkey."

"Did I hurt anyone?"

"No."

"Well, let me go," Bob said. "I'm hungry, and my head hurts. I need a drink."

"A drink's the last thing you need," Mitch said. "When did you last see George Orr?"

"George? He's my partner," said Bob.

"When did you last see him?"

"When I left the mine to come into town," said Bob. "Why?"

"Was he alive?"

"Well, sure he was alive. Why? What are you getting at?"

"George Orr is dead," said Mitch.

"Dead? George? How?"

"Someone bashed in his head out at your shack," Mitch said. "You don't know anything about it, I guess."

"No, I—George? Dead? I don't know nothing about it," Bob said. "He was all right when I seen him last. Let me go, Sheriff. Hell, I'm sober now."

"You can stand it a while longer," Mitch said. "I'll have some food and coffee sent over to you."

He left Bob sitting in the dirt and walked over to Ellie's "Eat Here" establishment. He ordered himself a bowl of beef stew and some corn bread and a cup of coffee and asked

Ellie to have the same thing sent over to the jail for Big Bob. He was sipping his coffee and waiting for his stew when Jewel Reid walked up to his table. "Hello, Sheriff," she said. "Mind if I join you?"

Mitch looked up at her and then looked around. There were plenty of other places to sit. He shrugged. "Suit yourself," he said. She was a pretty girl. There was no question about that, but she was Reid's daughter, and he had no desire to be better acquainted with her. She sat down, and Ellie approached with Mitch's meal. "Coffee," Jewel said.

"Anything to eat?" Ellie asked her.

"No, thanks," said Jewel. "Just coffee. I've already eaten."

Mitch slurped up a bite of stew. He looked at Jewel, wondering what she was up to.

"How're things going for you?" she asked him.

Mitch swallowed and glanced up at her. She really looked lovely. Had she had any other father in the world, he'd have been thrilled to have her company. "Got a killing to investigate," he said.

"I heard," she said. "Do you have any suspects?"

"Too many," Mitch said.

"You don't talk much, do you?" Jewel said. "Is that because you're Indian?"

"It's because I've got nothing to say," Mitch answered.

"You don't like me, do you?" she said.

"It's got nothing to do with you," Mitch said.

"What, then?" she asked. "Do you just not like people? White people? Or don't you like women?"

"I guess I ain't got much use for most folks," Mitch admitted. "It don't matter what color they are. And I guess I like women as much as most men."

"Then what is it about me?" she said. "I just sat down to be friendly. That's all. Just to have a friendly visit."

"You really want to know?" said Mitch. "Well, all right. I'll tell you, damn it. It's your old man. He's forced me to stay on here and be the sheriff. He's a back-stabbing, double-dealing son of a bitch. That's what it is."

51

"What do you mean?" she asked, incredulous. "How could he force you to stay here? How could he force you to be the sheriff?"

"I can't tell you that part," Mitch said. "But it's true. What's more, you asked me about my suspects. Well, he's one of them. He's at the top of the list."

"You're not only unfriendly," Jewel said, standing up, "you're also crazy."

She turned sharply and flounced out of the tent, leaving Mitch to finish his meal alone. He was relieved, but he was also agitated. He hadn't asked for her company. She had imposed herself on him and thoroughly spoiled his meal. Pressing him with questions, then calling him names. Damn her and her son-of-a-bitch father. Damn them both and their damn town. Damn them all to hell.

When Mitch got back to his office, he found Reid waiting there for him. He should have expected it, he told himself. She had run right to Daddy and told him everything. Well, that was all right. He didn't give a damn, he told himself. What could Reid do to him that he hadn't already done?

"You're sitting in my chair, Mr. Reid," he said.

Reid stood up and walked out from behind the desk. He gestured toward the chair, and Mitch went to it and sat. "What the hell do you want?" he said.

"I hear that you just had a fight with my daughter," Reid said.

"I wouldn't have called it that," said Mitch. "She slung some insults at me, but she never hit me."

"You told her that I'm at the top of your list of suspects for the killing of George Orr," said Reid. "You want to tell me about it?"

"All right," Mitch said. "Sit down. Let's have a talk."

Reid pulled a chair up to the desk and sat facing Mitch. Mitch rolled himself a smoke and lit it. He offered the makings to Reid, who, instead of accepting them, reached into his coat pocket for an expensive cigar. "I prefer these," he said.

"You told me that Duncklee killed a man out at your mine office," Mitch said. "Said he bashed the man's head in with a shovel."

"That's right," said Reid. "He stole the mine's payroll. You ought to know. You brought back the money."

"He had the money, all right," Mitch said. "It just seems kind of peculiar that another miner's got his head bashed in now. It makes me wonder if the same man might have done both killings. If that's so, then it sure wasn't Duncklee."

"Then how did he get the money?" Reid asked.

"Maybe someone else bashed out the brains of— What was the name of the man you claim Duncklee killed?"

"Howard Jones," said Reid.

Mitch wrote the name down on a piece of paper. "Maybe someone bashed in Jones's head for whatever reason, and then Duncklee come along and found him like that. With the money there and no one to stop him, maybe he just took the money and run off. Now whoever it was done the killing has struck again."

"And you think it was me?" said Reid. Mitch shrugged. "Why?" Reid added. "What's my motive? For either one?"

"I don't know that," said Mitch. "Yet. You want to show me your boot soles?"

Reid grinned and lifted both his feet off the floor to plop them down on top of Mitch's desk. Mitch took a good look. They didn't match with any of the prints he had found around the shack where Orr had been killed. He hadn't really expected them to.

"Well?" Reid said.

"I don't really expect that you'd go around bashing heads in," said Mitch. "Hiring it done is more your style."

"So I'm at the top of your list," Reid said. "Who else is on the list?"

"Big Bob," Mitch said. "I don't really think he done it, but he could have. He says he left Orr alive. But with his partner dead, he'll likely own all the gold out at their place. Course, I'll have to check that out. Be sure that Orr didn't leave his share to someone else."

"I'll check that out for you," Reid said. "Who else?"

"Manny," said Mitch. "Just because he found the body. He has to be on the list, but I don't think it was him either. There's one unidentified set of footprints and one unidentified set of horse tracks out there. I'll be watching for a match to either set."

Reid dropped his feet to the floor and stood up.

"Well," he said, "you seem to be following all the right steps. I knew you were the right man for this job. Keep up the good work, and keep me informed. Will you?"

"I will," Mitch said.

"Oh, and, uh, it's just as well that you didn't get on well with Jewel," Reid said. "I'd much rather she not be hanging around with you."

Chapter Seven

Mitch sat in his office making notes. He wrote down the names of George Orr and Howard Jones, both murdered within a few days, both with their heads bashed in from behind. He wished that he had been able to examine the body of Jones the way it had been found. As far as Reid was concerned, the Jones case was closed. Reid had said that Duncklee was the killer of Jones, and Duncklee had been in possession of the missing money. There was no question about that. It would have been comforting to Mitch if he could have believed that Duncklee was the murderer, but the similarity of the two killings had given him doubts.

Off to the right side of the paper, he started a list of names—his suspects. The name of J. Paxton Reid headed the list, but next to Reid's name he wrote the word "why?" Underneath Reid's name, he listed the names of Manny Gordon and Big Bob McNamara. He wrote the same note beside Manny's name as he had beside Reid's, but beside the name of Big Bob, he wrote, "the gold mine." He scratched his head in puzzlement and realized that he had a lot of work to do. He got up and walked out back, where he found Big Bob just finishing up his stew. He reached down to unlock the padlock that held Big Bob in his chain.

"Come with me," he said. Bob stood up, stretched, moaned, and followed Mitch into the office. "Have a chair," said Mitch. Bob sat in the chair across the desk from Mitch.

"Can I go?" he said.

"Not just yet," said Mitch. "I have a few questions for you. You said that when you left your partner, he was alive."

"Well, yeah," said Bob. "Sure he was. He was cooking himself some meat. I told him I was going to town, and he just said he'd see me later. That's all."

"You came into town just to get drunk?" Mitch asked.

Bob hung his head. "Well, yeah," he said. "I reckon."

"Did Orr ever come to town to drink with you?"

"No," said Bob. "He didn't drink none."

"Did Orr have any heirs?"

"What?"

"Did he leave his share of your mine to anyone?" Mitch asked. "Any relatives?"

"Oh," said Bob. "No. Our papers just said that if anything was to happen to one of us the other one gets everything. That's—Wait a minute. I get it. You think that I killed George for the mine. Is that it? Well, I never. Me and George was partners. And there was plenty of gold. We was doing real well, we was. Why would I kill George?"

"For some men, there's never enough gold," Mitch said. "Getting some just makes them want more."

"Well, not me," said Bob, standing up. "I never killed George. I left him alive out at the shack, and that's all. You find out who really done it. You find out and leave me alone."

"Who else had a reason to kill George?" Mitch asked.

"I don't know," Bob said. "Everybody liked George. The only reason anyone would kill George would be to rob us of our gold."

"I found your gold still in the shack," Mitch said. "It's still there."

"Well, maybe whoever done it couldn't find the gold after he killed George," Bob said.

"It didn't look to me like anyone had ever searched the shack," Mitch said. "I don't think it was a thief who killed him. At least not that kind of a thief."

"Well, it wasn't me," Bob said. "Can I go now? Do I have to pay a fine or something?"

"Go on," said Mitch, "but I suggest you go back to your mine. If you get drunk again, I'll just chain you up again, and I'll get you longer the next time."

George started to leave, then hesitated. "Can I have my gun back?" he asked.

Mitch opened a desk drawer and pulled out the revolver and its belt and holster. He handed it across the desk to Bob. "It ain't loaded," he said.

Bob took it and hurried out of the office. Mitch looked back down at his notes and focused on the possible motive written beside the name of Big Bob. "The gold mine," it said. He put the notes in a drawer, then shoved his chair back and stood up. He left the office and walked over to Reid's office. When he walked in, Reid looked up, surprised to see him again so soon.

"I want to go out to your mine," said Mitch. "I want to see where Jones's body was found, and I want to talk to whoever it was that found him there."

"I think you're on the wrong track there, Mitch," said Reid, "but come on. I'll take you out there."

The Paxton mine was a big operation, with tracks for mining cars coming out of a deep shaft on the side of a mountain. The main mining shack was perched precariously on the mountain's side, and the trail up to it was steep. Mitch and Reid left their mounts a little below the shack, then walked up a narrow, winding stairway to the door. Reid opened the door and stepped aside, indicating with a gesture that Mitch should precede him into the operations office. Mitch stepped in and aside to allow Reid to follow.

There were two desks and several chairs. Filing cabinets stood against the walls, as well as a large safe. The door to the safe was closed. A man sat behind one of the desks. He looked up as the two other men came into the room.

"Carson," said Reid, "this is Mitch Frye. He's the new sheriff of Paxton. Mitch, this is Bill Carson. He's the manager out here."

"Glad to meet you, Sheriff," said Carson.

"Yeah," Mitch said. "Who found Jones?"

"I did," said Carson.

"Tell me about it," Mitch said.

"Well," said Carson, "Jones had the night shift here. I came in about eight in the morning to take over, and he was lying there on the floor. I could see right away that he was dead. His skull was all crushed in."

"Just exactly where was the body?" Mitch asked.

"Right over here," said Carson, walking toward the safe and indicating a spot on the floor.

"On his face or on his back?" Mitch asked.

"On his face."

"Which way was his head?"

"Right over there." Carson indicated that Jones's body had been lying facedown, the head near the safe and the feet toward the door.

"Then whoever killed him," Mitch said, "was right up close behind him. About here."

Carson gave Reid a curious look. "Duncklee did it," he said. "Didn't he?"

"The sheriff's not sure about that," said Reid. "Someone killed old George Orr just the same way. Duncklee was already dead when that happened."

"Oh," said Carson.

"Tell me, Carson," Mitch said, "was the safe open or closed?"

"It was standing open," Carson said. "That was the next thing I noticed. I knew that the payroll had been in there, so

I looked in right away and saw that it was missing. Duncklee worked with Jones at night, and since I didn't see him anywhere, I hurried on into town and told Mr. Reid about it. We never did find Duncklee, so we just naturally assumed that he had killed Jones and run away with the payroll.''

"Well, he ran away, all right," Mitch said, "and he had the money. Who had the combination to the safe?"

"Well," Carson said, "there was me and Jones. Duncklee had it, and, of course, Mr. Reid."

"Anyone else?"

"No," said Carson, glancing toward Reid.

"No one," Reid confirmed.

"Once that payroll money had been locked in the safe," Mitch asked, "is there any reason either Jones or Duncklee would have to open the safe again in the middle of the night?"

"If they were working on the books," Carson mused, "they might have needed to get some books out, or maybe if they'd finished some figuring, they might have been putting the books back."

"The books were kept in the safe too?" said Mitch.

"Right," Carson answered.

"So maybe Jones was getting ready to put the books back in the safe," Reid volunteered, "and when Duncklee saw it open and the money right there to be had, he was overcome. He bashed Jones in the head and took the money."

"It might have happened like that," Mitch agreed. "But then, it might have been someone other than Duncklee who did the killing."

"Who else could it have been?" Reid demanded.

"Whoever killed Orr," said Mitch.

Reid said he had some business to talk over with Carson, so Mitch started back down the road alone. He could see why Reid was said to own the town of Paxton. Mitch had seen only one other mine, that of the late George Orr and Big Bob McNamara, but it was tiny compared to Reid's. He wondered what the others were like, and he decided that soon he would find a way of making a tour to see them all. He had gotten himself familiar with the town, and for a while he had thought that would be enough. Now, though, he felt like he needed to be more familiar with all the surrounding mines.

He was about halfway back to town when he found the road blocked by four mounted men. Each man had the look of a hard ruffian. Each man had a stern expression on his face. One man held a shotgun at the ready. Mitch moved his horse over close to the mountain wall that rose high above in order to make room for the riders to pass him by on the narrow road. None of them made a move.

"You got something on your mind?" Mitch asked.

"Yeah," said one of the riders, a large man with a red beard. "You."

"What about me?" Mitch said.

"We want you to ride out of town," red beard said.

"I can't do that," said Mitch. "I've got a job."

"You can quit your job and ride out," said red beard. "There's folks in Paxton who don't take kindly to having a damned Apache with a badge lording it over them."

"Is that right?" Mitch said. "What folks would they be? You four?"

"Us four," said red beard, "and others."

"Take it up with the mayor," said Mitch. "Right now, get out of my way."

The man with the shotgun moved it slightly so that it was leveled at Mitch. Mitch knew that there was no arguing with a shotgun.

"We'll get out of your way," red beard said, "after we've done a little convincing on you."

Chapter Eight

The dirty man with the shotgun, the smallest of the four, grinned and showed ugly yellow teeth. "Keep your hands up away from your gun," he said, "or I'll cut you in half."

Red beard dismounted, followed by the other two. Red beard walked over to Mitch's side, reached up, and pulled Mitch's Colt out of its holster. Then he tossed it aside. He reached up as if to grab Mitch, but Mitch slipped his foot out of the stirrup and shoved him, knocking him to the ground. The other two ran for Mitch as he tried to kick his horse into a run, but hands grabbed at him from both sides. Red beard was back on his feet, and he joined them. Soon they had dragged Mitch out of the saddle and had him on the ground. They were pounding him with fists and kicking him in the face and in the ribs. Even the yellow-toothed one had put down his shotgun to join in the fun.

Mitch managed to get in a few good punches and kicks, but the four were too much for him. At last a hard kick to the side of his head knocked him unconscious. When he

61

came to, he had no idea how long he had been there in the road. He wondered if anyone had come by. If so, they had just ignored him and let him lie there. The four ruffians were nowhere in sight. Mitch sat up slowly. He hurt all over. He touched the side of his head, and he could tell that blood was crusted there. He started to get up to his feet, and pain shot through his body. Broken ribs, he told himself.

He did manage to get up to his feet, though, and he saw that his horse was still not far away. He looked around for his Colt and found it just off the side of the road. A little harder toss from red beard would have sent it down the side of the mountain. He retrieved it and holstered it. Then he walked painfully to his patient horse and with considerable difficulty got himself back into the saddle.

Riding back toward town, Mitch wondered if Reid was still out at the mine. He thought that it had been awfully convenient for Reid to have ridden out to the mine with him, then found a reason to stay, thereby allowing the four men to catch him alone on the road. But if Reid wanted Mitch out of town, all he had to do was give up that incriminating paper that Mitch had signed. He didn't have to resort to setting ruffians on him. Reid knew that Mitch wanted nothing more than to leave town. Still, he couldn't help being suspicious of Reid.

He pulled up in front of his office, dismounted, and lapped the reins around the hitching rail. He walked slowly and painfully toward his office door, but before he reached it, Jewel Reid came running up to his side. He didn't see where she had come from.

"What happened to you?" she asked.

"I run into some Indian haters," Mitch said. "I'll live."

He started to go on into the office, but Jewel put an arm around his waist. "Here," she said. "Let me help. Lean on me."

"I'm all right," said Mitch, but Jewel stayed with him. Together they went back to Mitch's living quarters, and she helped him to lie down on his bed. Then she found a towel, wet it in the water bowl, and sat down on the edge of the bed to wash his face. He winced at the touch, but he didn't argue with her anymore. She cleaned him up as best she could, and then she told him to rest and wait right there until she returned. Again he didn't argue. She left, and in a few minutes she came back with medicine and bandages.

She made him take off his shirt, and she wrapped his ribs up tight. Then she dabbed ointment on the cuts on his head and face. He was still trying not to like her. He wanted to not like her because of her father, and now he also knew that her father wanted him to stay away from her. Why? Because he was Apache? Because he was a man-killer? It didn't really matter much. The point was that Mitch didn't want to have anything to do with Jewel Reid, but she had caught him at a weak and vulnerable time, and she had helped him. He was feeling better since she had nursed his cuts and bruises and wrapped his ribs. He was grateful. He wanted to be rude and run her off, but he was too grateful. And her touch had been . . . well, it had been nice.

He started to lie back on the bed again, but she stopped him. "You'd better stay up," she said. "After a kick in the head like you took, you shouldn't sleep. Here." She reached into the bag she had brought back with the bandages and ointment and such and pulled out a bottle of whiskey. She uncorked it and handed it to Mitch. "Drink some of this," she said.

"I don't ever drink this early in the day," Mitch said.

"This is medicine," she said. "Drink some."

Mitch took the bottle and turned it up for a long swallow. Then he handed it back to her. He had to admit to himself that it did seem to help clear his head some. "Thanks," he said.

"Is there anything else I can do for you?" she asked.

"No," he said. "You've done plenty. I'm grateful to you."

"Tell me what happened," she said.

"There ain't much to tell," said Mitch. "I rode up to your daddy's mine with him, and when I got ready to come back to town, he stayed there. On the way down, I met four men

63

blocking the road. One of them was holding a shotgun on me, so there wasn't much I could do. They disarmed me and beat me up. That's all.''

"Did they say why?" she asked.

"Said they wanted me to leave town. They don't like having an Apache sheriff.''

"The cowards," she said. "Do you know who they were?"

"I don't recall ever seeing them before," Mitch said. "The ringleader was a big man with a red beard.''

Jewel wrinkled her brow in thought. "It could have been Red Calhoun," she said. "It sounds like something he might have said and done.''

"Red Calhoun," Mitch repeated, to set the name in his mind. "Who's he?"

"He's one of the small miners," Jewel said. "Beyond that, he's a bully and a troublemaker. He's never been caught at anything downright illegal, though.''

"Well," Mitch said, "he has now."

Mitch wanted to lie down and sleep, but Jewel wouldn't let him. Instead she made him walk over to Ellie's tent and get something to eat and drink some coffee. He grumbled about it, but he knew she was right. He'd seen plenty of victims of blows to the head in his years with the scouts, so, grumbling or not, he allowed her to lead him around. And as before, he felt a little better after he had taken her advice.

He finished his meal and several cups of coffee, all of which went on the town tab, and he got up to leave. Jewel took hold of his arm. "You're not going back to your room to sleep?" she said.

"No," he said. "I'm going over to your daddy's office and see if he's back yet.''

"I'll go with you," she said.

"I think it'd be better if you didn't," said Mitch.

"Why?"

"Well," he said, "I just think it would. Don't worry about me. I won't go back and go to sleep. I promise.''

Reluctantly, she let him go. He left her there standing just

GET YOUR 4
FREE* BOOKS NOW—
A VALUE BETWEEN
$16 AND $20

Mail the Free* Book Certificate Today!

FREE* BOOKS
CERTIFICATE!

YES! I want to subscribe to the Leisure Western Book Club. Please send me my 4 FREE* BOOKS. Then, each month, I'll receive the four newest Leisure Western Selections to preview FREE* for 10 days. If I decide to keep them, I will pay the Special Member's Only discounted price of just $3.36 each, a total of $13.44 ($14.50 US in Canada). This saves me between $3 and $6 off the bookstore price. There are no shipping, handling or other charges.* There is no minimum number of books I must buy and I may cancel the program at any time. In any case, the 4 FREE* BOOKS are mine to keep—at a value of between $17 and $20!

*In Canada, add $5.00 Canadian shipping and handling per order for first shipment. For all subsequent shipments to Canada the cost of membership in the Book Club is $14.50 US, which includes $7.50 shipping and handling per month. All payments must be made in US currency.

Name _____

Address _____

City_____ State____ Country_____

Zip_____ Telephone_____

Tear here and mail your FREE* book card today!

Get Four Books Totally FREE* – A Value between $16 and $20

Tear here and mail your FREE* book card today!

PLEASE RUSH
MY FOUR FREE*
BOOKS TO ME
RIGHT AWAY!

LeisureWestern Book Club
P.O. Box 6613
Edison, NJ 08818-6613

AFFIX
STAMP
HERE

outside the door to Ellie's tent café, and he walked over to Reid's office. He saw the horse standing at the hitching rail outside, so he knew that Reid was back. He went on inside, through the outer office, and stopped at the door to Reid's private office. Reid looked up from behind his desk and saw Mitch standing there.

"Good God," he said, coming up to his feet and walking around the desk to meet Mitch. "What the hell happened to you?"

"Some Paxton citizens met me along the road back," Mitch said. "They don't like Apaches—especially Apaches wearing a sheriff's badge."

"Who were they?" Reid demanded.

"I never saw them before," said Mitch. He thought that he shouldn't let on to Reid that he had been talking to Jewel. "One of them, the one who did all the talking, was a big man with a red beard."

"Red Calhoun," Reid said.

"Where do I find him?" Mitch asked.

"You don't want to go after him right now," Reid said.

"No," Mitch said. "I'll wait a bit. My ribs are pretty sore right now. Just tell me where I can find him."

"He has a mine on beyond Big Bob's," Reid said. "When you're ready, I'll take you up there."

"I'd rather you just draw me a map," said Mitch, "showing where all the mines are around here. I'll go out and visit them on my own. Does this Red Calhoun have any special cronies he hangs out with?"

"You said there were four of them?" Reid asked.

"That's right," said Mitch. "Besides the red beard, there was a little whiny bastard with yellow teeth. He was toting a shotgun. The other two was about the same size as Red, but both of them had dark hair—I think. Scruffy-looking beards."

"It could be Hammerhead, Dog, and Crazy Karl," Reid said. "That is, if the red-bearded one was Calhoun, like I suspect. Those four hang together quite a bit."

"Are they all miners?" Mitch asked.

"Red's the only one I know of that's a miner," Reid said. "At least, he has a claim filed, and he lives on it. I'm not convinced that he does any actual mining. The other three just kind of hang around. I've suspected them of several robberies we've had around here, but there's never been any proof."

"Sounds like they'll be worth checking into," Mitch said. "I'll see if I feel up to it in the morning."

"Well, take care of yourself," said Reid. "You won't be any good to me if you get yourself knocked clear out of commission."

"What about that map of the mines?"

Reid drew out a map, and Mitch took it back to his office to study. In a short while he had the layout pretty well set in his mind. When he got ready to go out scouting, he told himself, he'd carry the map along anyhow—just in case. At last he decided that he'd been up and around long enough. It would be safe to go to bed. He locked the front door and went back to his room. Stretching out slowly and carefully on his bed, he soon fell into a deep sleep.

Chapter Nine

It was noon the next day when Mitch had Sam Neely saddle his horse. Then he climbed up into the saddle. It was still a painful chore, but he managed it, and with the map of the surrounding mines drawn by Reid in his pocket, he started on his slow and easy tour. He met Herman Connolly, a grumpy little man, at the Hambone, a small, one-man operation. From there he rode back up to the Paxton and stopped in to see Carson and ask how things were going.

"What did Reid have to hang around for yesterday?" he asked.

"I don't know," Carson said. "He looked some at the books and made some small talk. Actually, he didn't do much but keep me from my work."

Mitch thought that over while he was riding on to the next place, Big Bob's. He found Big Bob hard at work. Bob looked up when he saw Mitch. "What do you want?" he said. His tone was not friendly. Mitch stayed in his saddle. It had hurt enough getting down at the Paxton and then getting back up, but at the Paxton he'd had no choice.

"I'm just riding by," Mitch said. "Got a couple of questions for you."

"Well?" said Big Bob.

"Did you find anything missing when you came back up here?"

"No," Bob said.

"Had any ideas since we talked about who might have killed your partner?"

"No."

"Do you know a man called Red Calhoun?"

"I know him," said Bob, and he spat. "Son of a bitch."

"You don't like him?" Mitch asked.

"He's no good," said Bob. "Him and his pals. They just hang around making trouble. They don't work."

"What kind of trouble?"

Bob gave a shrug. "I don't know. They like to push people around. Start fights. They rob people, too. I never seen it. Can't prove it, but they've always got money, and they don't work."

"Have you had any run-ins with them?" Mitch asked. "You or your partner?"

"I had a fight with them once," Bob admitted. "They beat me up, but it took all four of them. But if you're thinking that they might have killed George, you're thinking wrong. If they had done it, the gold would be gone. Besides, they never had no trouble with George."

"Who are the other three men?"

"I don't know their real names," Bob said. "I don't think no one knows them."

"What are they called?"

"Hammerhead, Crazy Karl, and Dog," Bob said.

"Thanks," said Mitch, and he turned his horse and rode off. Mitch pulled the map out of his pocket and checked it as he rode. The next stop was a place called the Lucky Hole. The owner, Mike Priber, was not around. Mitch rode on to Red Calhoun's small mine, registered simply as Calhoun's. He approached the place slowly. A lone horse stood in the small corral just outside the shack. Mitch drew out his Colt as he rode up close to the shack. No one came out to challenge him. He called out.

"Calhoun, you in there?"

There was no response. Cursing mildly, Mitch grabbed hold of the saddle horn and swung himself out of the saddle with a groan. He walked over to the door and knocked. "Calhoun," he called out again. Still there was no answer. Cautiously, he opened the door. For a moment he could see nothing in the dark interior of the small shack. He stepped inside and discovered Red Calhoun sprawled facedown on the floor. The back of his head was caved in.

Mitch rode back into Paxton leading Calhoun's horse, with the remains of the red-bearded man slung across its saddle. He stopped in front of Reid's office, and Reid stepped out onto the board sidewalk.

"That looks like Red Calhoun," Reid said.

"That's who it used to be," said Mitch. Wincing with the pain, he dismounted.

"Did you have to kill him?" Reid asked.

"I didn't kill him," said Mitch. "I found him in his shack—just like George Orr."

"I'll be damned," Reid said. "I can think of a dozen men who'd want to kill Red, you included, but who would want to kill George Orr?"

"And Jones," Mitch added.

"I still think Duncklee killed Jones," said Reid.

"Three bashed-in skulls at mine shacks add up to something," said Mitch.

"Yeah, but what?" Reid said.

"Will you get this taken care of?" Mitch asked, nodding toward the body.

"I'll see to it," said Reid, and Mitch started walking toward his own office, leading his horse. Back behind his desk, he pulled out his notes. He added the name of Red Calhoun to the list of victims. He thought for a moment, then began another list. "All had heads bashed in from behind," he wrote. "All killed in mine shacks," he added under that. He

69

thought for another moment, then wrote, "Likely they knew the killer." But then, he thought, neither Red nor George had been robbed. Both Red and George were small-mine owners. Jones had been an employee of a large mine, and the safe had been robbed there. He wondered if Reid could possibly be right. Could Duncklee have killed Jones, and someone else killed the other two?

Mitch shoved the paper back into a desk drawer, got up, and walked out back to check on the progress of the new jail. The walls were almost complete. They would be putting a roof on it soon. There was one window, and, of course, it wasn't barred. He still had his chain and padlock, though, and he wished that he had a murderer to lock up. As he stood there, one of the men stopped working and stepped over close to Mitch, wiping his brow on a sleeve.

"What do you think, Sheriff?" he said.

"I reckon it'll do," said Mitch, "once it's finished. What are you going to do about that window?"

"Oh, it'll have bars," the man said. "Mr. Reid said he'd get them."

Then Mitch recognized the man. It was the same man he had spoken to in the street on his first day in Paxton. "Say, I know you," he said. "You were the first friendly voice I heard in this town. Still one of the few." He held out his hand. "I'm Mitch Frye."

"I know," the man said, taking Mitch's hand for a firm shake. "I'm Jasper Boone."

"Pleased to make it formal," Mitch said. "What do you do around here when you're not building jails?"

Jasper shrugged. "Odd jobs," he said. "Mostly building. Like everyone else around, I came out looking for gold. I didn't have as much luck as some. Finally gave it up."

"You're probably better off for it," Mitch said. "How long before the jail's done?"

"Three, maybe four more days," Jasper said. "That is, if I get back to work and help these guys."

Mitch smiled. "Nice visiting with you," he said. Jasper

turned back to his work, and Mitch went back through the building to his office.

He pulled the paper out of his desk drawer again and studied it, hoping that he would notice something he had failed to take note of before. Some connection between the murdered men, some clue that he had overlooked. But nothing came to him. The killer, or killers, had been known to all three victims, for all three men had obviously turned their backs on the killer with the killer close by in the room. All three victims were miners; two were mine owners. All three had been bashed in the head from behind.

In the case of Jones at the Paxton, one hundred thousand dollars had been stolen, but in the other two cases there was no evidence of anything having been taken or disturbed. Mitch still could not get the idea out of his mind that someone other than Duncklee had killed Jones, and that Duncklee had come along later and found the man dead, then stolen the money. He also could not get it out of his mind that Reid had something to do with the killings. Even so, he had to ask himself if he just wanted Reid to have something to do with them.

Then there was the matter of Red Calhoun's three companions with the peculiar nicknames: Dog, Crazy Karl, and Hammerhead. Mitch did not think that they had anything to do with the killings, but he wanted to find them and arrest them for assaulting an officer of the law. He knew that he wouldn't be worth a damn as a lawman if he let them get away with what they had done. He decided that since he had no idea where to turn on the matter of the murders, he might just as well go after the three bullies. He thought that he would make the rounds of the saloons, and if he didn't happen on them that way, he'd start asking questions about them.

In the third saloon, Mitch saw one of the three men standing alone at the bar. He walked over to stand beside the man. When he noticed that he was being crowded, the man turned to face Mitch, recognizing him immediately.

"You," he said, reaching for the revolver at his side.

Mitch grabbed the man's wrist with his left hand and smacked him a good hard cross with his right. Then before the wretch could recover from the blow, Mitch twisted his right arm around behind him in a tight hammerlock. "Ahh! Ahh! You're breaking my arm!" he cried.

"That's not a bad idea," said Mitch. He took the revolver out of the man's holster, cocked it, then released his arm. Training the man's own revolver on him, he said, "Let's go."

"Where to?" said the man, wincing and rubbing his left arm.

"Jail," said Mitch.

"This town ain't got a jail," the man said.

"There's a new one going up," Mitch said. "March."

As he marched his prisoner out of the saloon, Mitch took note of the number of customers. The saloon wasn't as crowded as the first two had been, but there were enough men in there to make him believe that the word of the man's arrest would get back to his friends soon enough. That was what he was hoping for. Let them come to him. It would save him a lot of searching.

At the still-unfinished jail, Mitch chained his prisoner to the log where he had kept Big Bob before. "What the hell is this?" the man said.

"I told you the jail ain't finished," Mitch said. "But that'll hold you. Which one are you, anyway?"

"Which one what?" the man said.

"What's your name?" Mitch demanded in a sterner tone.

"They call me Dog," the man said.

"That's appropriate," said Mitch.

"It's what?"

"It suits you."

"Go to hell, you son of a bitch," Dog said.

"You'll be there long before me, you yellow dog," Mitch said.

"You can't keep me here," Dog said. "Red and Crazy Karl and Hammerhead will come for me. This time we'll kill you, you goddamned redskin."

72

"I guess you ain't heard the news," Mitch said. "Karl and Hammerhead will have to try to do the job by themselves. Someone killed Red."

"What?" said Dog. "Killed him? Who? Not you?"

"Whoever it was got there ahead of me," Mitch said. "Bashed in his skull from behind. Just like Jones and Orr. You heard about them, didn't you?"

"I heard about them, all right," Dog said. "But not Red."

"Well," said Mitch, "Red's the latest. You know anything about those killings?"

"Me? Hell no. I don't know nothing about them. Only thing I heard was that Duncklee done the first one. That's all."

"What happens to Red's mine, now that he's dead?" Mitch asked.

Dog gave a shrug. "I don't know," he said. "He never said nothing about that. Not to me."

"All right," Mitch said, and he turned to walk away.

"Hey," Dog shouted. "Wait a minute. You ain't leaving me here like this, are you?"

"You're in jail," said Mitch without bothering to look back at Dog. He continued his way back into his office building.

"You son of a bitch," Dog shouted. "My friends will kill you for this. They'll kill you, you son of a bitch."

73

Chapter Ten

Mitch sat down at his desk to make a note on the arrest. For the prisoner's name he wrote, "Dog." The man must have more name than that, he thought. Then he thought about Hammerhead and Crazy Karl. At least Big Bob and Red both had last names, but, he thought, they might not be their real names. He recalled, while making his rounds in the saloons, that a drunk had been singing a song the refrain of which was, "What was your name in the states?" That made him wonder about Jones too. Jones was a common alias. Duncklee and Orr sounded more like real names, but one could never tell.

It seemed that quite a few of the men in this town were going around under assumed names. Why? Because they had done something back where they came from that they didn't want to caught for? Because they were fugitives of some kind? From the law? From a wife? And then it occurred to Mitch that if he knew what the real names of the murder victims were, perhaps he could figure out what it was they had in common—more, that is, than what he had already figured.

He decided to have another talk with Reid, so he walked over and found the mayor in his office. "What's on your mind?" Reid asked him as he walked in.

"Names," said Mitch, taking a chair.

"Names?" Reid echoed.

"Names like Hammerhead, Crazy Karl, Dog, Red, Big Bob, and Jones," Mitch said. "And others. Duncklee and George Orr. Like the song asks, 'What were their names in the states?' Do you know anything about any of those men before they rode into Paxton?"

Reid shook his head. "We don't ask questions of a man when he comes to town," he said.

"Not even the men who work in your mine?"

"No. Not even them."

"You told me that Duncklee was some kind of an engineer," Mitch said. "How did you know that?"

"He told me," Reid said.

"And you gave him an important job on his say-so?"

"He seemed to know what he was talking about," said Reid. "I hired him and watched him for a few days. He seemed to know what he was doing. What are you getting at, anyway?"

"Maybe nothing," Mitch said, standing up. "I'm going to take another ride out to the sites of the killings."

"You think you can find anything more?" Reid asked.

"I might have overlooked something," said Mitch. He walked out of the office without another word.

"You again," Big Bob growled as Mitch rode up to his shack. "What do you want this time?"

Mitch eased himself down out of his saddle with a quiet moan. "I've got a few questions about your partner," he said.

"What do you want to know?"

"How long have you known him?" Mitch asked.

"We met in Denver," Big Bob said. "Maybe a year ago.

Maybe a little longer than that. I don't know. I didn't keep no records."

"Was he using the name George Orr when you met him?"

"Well, sure," Bob said. "What kind of a question is that?"

"Do you know if that was his real name?"

"It's the only one I ever heard of," said Bob.

"But you've only known him a year," Mitch said. "Do you know anything about his life before you met him?"

"I never asked no questions about that," said Bob. "I figured it wasn't none of my business."

"That seems to be the general attitude around here. Did he leave any personal effects?"

"Any what?"

"Any papers?" Mitch said. "Pictures? Anything like that?"

Big Bob turned his head toward the far wall, then pointed toward a box on the floor. "That there was his," he said.

"What's in it?" Mitch asked.

"I ain't looked," said Bob. "It wasn't none of my business."

Mitch walked over to the box and knelt beside it. He pulled off the lid and looked inside. There was an old navy Colt and a gold watch and, underneath, a stack of papers. He pulled the papers out, leaving the revolver and the watch in the box. Then, papers in one hand, the box in the other, he walked back across the room. He put the box on the table in front of Big Bob, then sat down on a bench with the papers in front of him.

"I guess those are yours," he said.

Bob took the gun and watch out of the box and held them, sitting quietly. Mitch started looking through the papers. He found a photograph of a woman and a letter from a woman who had signed, "Madge." He wondered if the photograph was of Madge. He read the letter and decided that Madge had been Orr's wife. She was waiting for him somewhere— waiting for him to come back home to Missouri after having made their fortune in the gold fields. The letter mentioned two children. It was addressed to George Orr, so that must have been the man's real name. Mitch passed the letter over to Big Bob.

"You might want to read this," he said. "You might want to write the lady and let her know what happened here."

Bob stared at the letter for a moment, then said, "I can't read nor write."

Mitch took the letter back and tucked it into his shirt. "I guess I'll write to her," he said with a sigh.

Mitch found nothing at Red Calhoun's shack, but back at Reid's office, he asked for any personal belongings that Jones had left behind. Reid produced a box. Like Orr's, it contained letters. They were all addressed to him under the name that he had used at Paxton. So far, Mitch thought, he had wasted his time on this trail. He still thought that he'd like to know what these men had done before they moved into the vicinity of Paxton. He would especially like to know if they had ever known each other before.

"Reid," he said, "you ever know the murder victims to hang out together?"

"No," Reid said, "and I still think you're barking up the wrong tree."

"You got any other ideas?" Mitch snapped. "Somebody's killing miners with no reason that we can see. There's got to be a reason. There's got to be a connection between these killings. You know of another way to look for one?"

Mitch made the rounds of the town, checking particularly the customers in the saloon, but he saw no sign of Crazy Karl or Hammerhead. It was getting late. Soon it would be dark. He walked back to his office and went through the building and out back to check on his prisoner.

"Still here, I see," he said.

"I'm going to tell Karl and Hammerhead not to kill you," Dog said. "I'm going to tell them to let me do it, and then I'm going to shoot you in the hands and the feet and the

77

knees and the elbows. And then I'm going to cut off your ears. Then maybe I'll kill you.''

Mitch turned to go back inside.

"Hey," Dog yelled. "I'm hungry. I ain't been fed.''

Mitch ignored his shouts and went on back to his office. He sat behind his desk waiting for the darkness to settle, thinking about the possible approach of Dog's pals. They could make a bold and direct frontal attack, but he doubted very much that they had the guts to do that. More likely, he thought, they'd sneak around back after dark and try to get Dog loose. They'd have a hard time of it, though.

Probably they would find that Dog was securely chained, wait until late when they thought that they'd be able to catch Mitch asleep, then try to sneak in and catch him off guard in order to get the keys. They might try to kill Mitch. They might just sneak off with the keys and wait for another time. After a while, he locked the front door, carried a chair with him to the back door, propped the chair against the door, and sat down to wait.

Mitch woke up with a start, realizing that it was beginning to get light. He wondered when he had dropped off to sleep, but more important, he wondered if Dog was still securely chained to the wall of the new jail outside. He jumped up to his feet, shoved the chair aside, and opened the door to look out. Dog was sleeping on the ground, still chained. Mitch walked over to him and kicked him in the butt with the side of his boot.

"Hey, yellow Dog," he said. "Wake up.''

Dog jumped, then slowly sat up, rubbing his eyes. "What?" he said. "What'd you do that for? Can't a man even sleep in jail?''

"How long do you reckon your good friends will let you sit here and starve?" said Mitch. "I ain't seen a sign of them.''

"They should've been here already," Dog whimpered.

"Maybe they ain't heard about your misfortune," said

Mitch. "If you'll tell me where to find them, I'll go give them the word."

"I ain't telling you nothing."

"Suit yourself," said Mitch.

"Wait a minute," Dog said. "You mean you'd hunt them up and tell them that you've got me locked up in jail?"

"Sure I would," said Mitch.

"Well, I don't know," Dog stammered. "I got to think on that."

"You afraid I'd just arrest them and bring them in?" Mitch asked. "It'd be two against one. Or do you and your kind need four-to-one odds like before?"

"They could handle you all right," Dog said.

"Then what do you need to think on?"

"All right, by God, I'll tell you," Dog said. "We stay in a shack up above the Paxton mine. It's an old mine shack, but the mine played out, so the miner just left it. We been staying up there."

"How come you didn't stay with Red?" said Mitch.

"Red was kind of funny about that," said Dog. "He didn't want no one staying at his place."

"Was Red Calhoun his real name?" Mitch asked.

"It's the only name I ever knowed him by," Dog answered.

"How long did you know him?"

"We all got together about six months ago," Dog said.

Mitch couldn't think of any more useful information he might get out of Dog, so he asked him for directions to the abandoned mine shack he and his cronies were using. Then, promising to send over a meal, he left his prisoner sitting in the dirt. He walked down to the stable and had Sam Neely saddle his horse. Then he rode out of town toward the Paxton mine.

Chapter Eleven

Mitch stopped at the Paxton mine office. As long as he was there he thought that he'd do a little further investigating. He asked if either Jones or Duncklee had left behind any personal belongings. There was nothing. He asked if anyone knew anything about the background of either man, but again, he got no satisfaction. He asked directions to the abandoned mine shack above the Paxton and received them. He rode on up there.

The trail was a blind one most of the way, with high rocks on either side. The thought came into Mitch's mind that he could be riding into an ambush, but then, he told himself, Hammerhead and Crazy Karl had no way of knowing that he was on the way. The trail ended at the shack, a wretched, dilapidated structure. He saw no horses or mules, no sign of the two men he was looking for. He stopped just in front of the shack and dismounted. Pain still shot through his body from the ribs that were either broken or badly bruised. He wasn't sure which.

He looked around carefully, then went inside the shack. It was dark in there, but no one was home. He waited for his eyes to adjust to the dim light, then began searching the place. He found empty bottles and full bottles. These men did not do all their drinking in town. He found a few tins of beans and some dirty dishes and pots. He found nothing that would tell him anything about the men who were squatting in the shack.

He was about to call it a wasted trip and head back toward town when he heard the sound of approaching horses' hoofs. He went outside and led his horse around to the side of the shack. Then he drew out his Colt and waited. Sure enough, Hammerhead and Crazy Karl rode up to the shack. Mitch didn't wait for them to dismount. He stepped out from around the corner of the shack, revolver in hand and cocked.

"Just sit still," he said.

"What do you want?" said the man with the yellow teeth.

"We'll start with your names," Mitch said.

"They call me Crazy Karl," said the yellow-toothed man.

"I'm Hammerhead," said the other. "How'd you find us up here?"

"Your friend Dog sent me," said Mitch. "Now, real careful, shuck those guns."

Hammerhead and Crazy Karl looked at each other, then each man pulled out his six-gun and dropped it to the ground. "Your long guns too," said Mitch. Hammerhead unsheathed a Marlin and dropped it. Reluctantly, Crazy Karl took a shotgun from his saddle and tossed it aside.

"What're you fixing to do to us?" Hammerhead asked.

"You're under arrest for assaulting an officer of the law," Mitch said. "Turn your horses around and start back down the trail. Go slow."

While Hammerhead and Crazy Karl turned their horses to head back down the trail, Mitch pulled his own mount out from the side of the shack and swung into the saddle. He did it quickly and tried to keep the pain from showing. He slipped the Colt back into its holster and pulled the Winchester out of its sheath, then chambered a shell. Hammerhead looked over his shoulder at the sound.

"If you try to run," Mitch said, "I can't hardly miss you with this."

"How long you think you can hold us in jail just for pounding on you the way we done?" Hammerhead called out.

"Long enough," Mitch said.

"Red and Dog will come after us," Crazy Karl yelled. "Then you'll wish you'd left things be."

"Dog's waiting for you in jail," Mitch said. "Red's dead."

"What's that?" Hammerhead said, hauling back on the reins to stop his horse. He turned in the saddle to face Mitch. "What happened?"

Mitch lifted his rifle barrel. "Keep moving," he said. Hammerhead started moving again, Crazy Karl still just in front of him on the narrow trail. "Someone bashed his head in for him over at his shack. Just like two other miners got it."

"Hell," said Hammerhead. "Red wasn't no miner. That mine wasn't no good anyhow. It was just a front."

"A front for what?" Mitch asked.

"Well, for, just for the hell of it, I guess," Hammerhead stammered. "He just wanted folks hereabouts to think he was a miner. That's all."

"Yeah? Well, where'd his money come from?"

Hammerhead gave a shrug. "He never told me," he said.

"How long you two known Red?"

"Maybe half a year," Hammerhead answered.

For an instant because of the curve of the narrow trail, Mitch lost sight of his prisoners. As he rounded the curve, Hammerhead leaned forward, hugging the neck of his horse. Crazy Karl, ahead of Hammerhead, had turned in his saddle and was pointing a pocket pistol at Mitch. Mitch dodged to one side as the tiny pistol cracked, then he fired his Winchester. Crazy Karl yelled and jerked in the saddle. Then he slumped. The pistol fell to the ground.

Mitch made Hammerhead dismount and drag the body of Crazy Karl out of the saddle, then load it so that it wouldn't fall off. Then he made Hammerhead remount his horse, ride ahead of the corpse-bearing horse, and lead it along. Back in Paxton, Mitch chained Hammerhead to the jail wall beside Dog. As he walked back toward the rear entrance of his office building, Dog whined out at him.

"Hey, you ever going to feed me?" He got no answer, and the tone of his voice changed to a snarl. "You Indian son of a bitch."

When Mitch got back into his office, he found Reid waiting there. "Seems like every time you ride out of town," Reid said, "someone winds up dead."

"Hello to you too," said Mitch.

"You kill Crazy Karl for helping to beat you up?" Reid asked.

"He pulled a gun on me," said Mitch. "He shot first. If I was killing them 'cause they beat me up, the other two wouldn't be in jail now, would they?"

"You call chaining them up like dogs putting them in jail?"

"You get my jail finished," said Mitch, "and I'll put them in proper. Till then I'll do what I have to do."

"Damn it, Mitch," Reid said, "all this killing looks bad."

"You don't like the way I'm doing my job," said Mitch, "you can always fire me. I'll be happy to ride on out of here."

"Fat chance," said Reid. He took a cigar out of his pocket and lit it with a wooden match. Then he sat down in the chair that faced Mitch across the desk. "What do you plan on doing with those boys out there?" he asked.

"Do we have a court and a judge in this town?" Mitch asked.

"No," said Reid. "We haven't made that much progress."

"Am I a real sheriff," Mitch asked, "or do I just work for you?"

"Your job's legal," Reid said. "I take it you're holding

them out there on a charge of assaulting an officer.''

"You take it right," Mitch said.

"Well, then," said Reid, puffing on his cigar, "hold them out there for a while—however long you think—and then turn them loose."

When Reid left the office, Mitch pulled out his notes on the murders again. He wrote the names Hammerhead, Crazy Karl, and Dog and put a big question mark beside them. Their pal Red had been one of the murder victims. It might not have anything to do with them, but then again, it might. They might know something. And then he asked himself another question. Did they ambush him and beat him up just because they hated Indians, or did they have some other reason to want him to leave town—like maybe to stop his investigation into the murders?

Chapter Twelve

Jewel Reid's entrance into the sheriff's office caught Mitch by surprise. He shoved his notes into a desk drawer as if he was afraid that she might see something that he wanted to keep a secret. He embarrassed himself with his haste. Standing up, he stammered a "hello" and indicated a chair.

"I hope I'm not interrupting anything," she said.

"No," he said. "Nothing. I was just . . . doing some thinking."

"About?" she said.

"What?" he said.

"What were you thinking about?" Jewel asked him, deciding to be more direct.

"Oh. Well, I wouldn't want to talk about it with a lady," he said. "It was law business."

"Was it those murders?" she asked him.

He looked at her, a little surprised. "Yeah," he said, taking the makings of a cigarette out of his shirt pocket. "I was puzzling over them." He curled a paper and poured tobacco into it. Then he closed the pouch by pulling the string with his teeth. He dampened an edge of the paper with the tip of his tongue, then deftly rolled the paper around the tobacco to form a neatly finished smoke. He stuck it in his mouth, reached for a match, struck it on the edge of his desk, and lit the cigarette. Exhaling a cloud of smoke, he said, "I can't make nothing out of it."

"Do you want to talk about it?" Jewel asked him.

"No," Mitch said, "it's my problem. I don't want to drag you in on it. It ain't a pleasant topic anyhow."

"I won't faint," Jewel said. "Besides, it might help to talk it out. What do you know?"

"That's the problem," Mitch said. "I don't know hardly nothing. What I know is that Jones, Orr, and Calhoun were all killed by a blow to the back of the head. Orr and Calhoun were both mine owners, and Jones worked at a mine. They don't seem to have nothing in common except mines. Calhoun's mine seems to have been a front of some kind. From everything I can find out, he wasn't really working it none. Orr and his partner, Big Bob, were digging out gold, all right, but there wasn't nothing stole from them. It seems like they ought to have something more in common, though."

"Why do you say that?" Jewel asked him.

"Because I think the same man killed them all," Mitch answered. He took a long drag on his cigarette and exhaled. "The same method was used in each case, and it seems to me like the victims all knew the killer. He was inside with them, and they each one turned their backs on him with him standing close by."

"Maybe he's crazy," Jewel said. "Maybe he's just someone who likes to go around bashing in heads."

"Then why's he doing it all at mine shacks?" Mitch asked. "Why ain't he killed someone in town?"

"Because the miners are all alone out there," she said. "Jones was working at Daddy's mine, but he was killed late at night when he was alone in the office. There's no one around. No witnesses."

Mitch sighed heavily. "It could be," he said. "But if

you're right about that, then I've even got a worse problem. If the killer's just a crazy man, then what do I look for?''

"What are you looking for now?" Jewel asked.

"Some connection between the dead men," said Mitch. "Like, did they know each other? No one around here can give me any connection, but did they maybe know each other before they come to Paxton? Hell, I don't even know if we got their real names."

Jewel chuckled a little. "Yeah," she said. "It's kind of common for men around here to use nicknames or aliases. We really don't know much about anyone. When a man rides into Paxton, no one asks about his background."

"I sure didn't count on nothing like this," Mitch said, shaking his head.

"What do you mean?" Jewel asked.

"When your old man . . . forced this job on me," he answered, "I figured it would be locking up drunks on Saturday night. Breaking up fights. Maybe chasing down a fugitive now and then. I didn't figure on having to try to figure out who's doing a string of killings."

"I doubt if anyone would have figured on that," said Jewel. "Whoever thinks that anything like that will take place right where they live?"

"Ah, I don't know," said Mitch. He walked over to the open window in the side wall of his office and tossed out his cigarette butt. "I don't know."

"Who benefits from the deaths of these men?" Jewel asked.

"I've been down that trail too," Mitch answered. "Big Bob owns the whole mine now, but I can't find out that anyone profits from Red Calhoun's death or from Jones'."

"So we have to find out who those men were before they came to Paxton," Jewel said, "and who knew them all?"

"What do you mean 'we'?" said Mitch.

"Just what I said. I intend to help you figure this out."

"This ain't something for you to be poking your nose in," Mitch said.

"I'll just ask some questions," she said. "That's all. If I

find out anything, I'll tell you. You want to take me to lunch?''

"Your old man wouldn't like it," Mitch said.

"So?" she said. "What'll he do about it? Fire you?"

"Let's go," said Mitch. "Ellie's?"

Billie Whitehead was alone at his mine. He had not been to town for almost a month, and no one had been out to see him. He liked it that way. He was a loner. He was very near to being a hermit. His claim was the farthest away from town, the farthest away from the other mines. There was no one really even close enough to call neighbor. Billie was down on his knees gouging between rocks with his knife—crevicing, it was called. He was deeply involved in his work, so the footsteps were close behind him before he heard them. He looked around quickly.

"Goddamn," he said. "What do you want to slip up on a man like that for?"

"I didn't slip up, Billie," the visitor said. "You're just getting hard of hearing or something. That's all."

Billie relaxed a little. "What the hell brings you all the way up here, anyhow?" he said.

"Ah, I didn't have anything to do," the man said. "I just thought I'd pay you a visit. See how things are going with you."

"I ain't found nothing," Billie said, but something about the way he said it and the way his eyes looked told a different story. The visitor chuckled. "I got nothing but blisters and a sore back out of this claim," Billie added.

"Hell," said the visitor, "that's the way it is, ain't it? Most never find any color. They dig for years, dig their lives away, and they never find anything. The ones that strike it rich, they're just a few. They're the ones we hear about. We know their names, and the reason we know them is because there're only a few of them. If every hard-rock miner struck it rich, we wouldn't remember any of them."

Billie just grunted. It was too much philosophizing for him.

"I haven't seen you in town for a spell," the visitor said. "That's the real reason I rode out here. I wanted to make sure you were all right."

"Ain't nothing wrong with me," Billie said. "I been working. That's all. I ain't got no reason to go to town. What the hell would I want to go to town for, anyhow?"

"Supplies?"

"I stocked up real good last time," Billie said.

"Get a drink."

"I don't hold with it."

"See a woman."

"They ain't nothing but trouble," Billie said. "I don't need none of that stuff you're talking about. When I get rich, I'm going to build me a mansion up on top of a mountain, and then I'm going to put a fence all around the base of the mountain. And there ain't going to be a town for a hundred miles in any direction."

Billie's visitor laughed. "What do you want to get rich for?" he asked.

"So I can buy the goddamned mountain," Billie said.

"Well, I guess you're all right," the visitor said. "I guess I can head on back to town. I don't suppose you'd offer me a cup of coffee before I go?"

"Aw, hell, why not," said Billie. "I could use a little myself. Come on inside, and I'll stoke up the fire."

Billie led the way into his small miner's shack. It was surprisingly neat, not what one would expect from a confirmed bachelor and misanthropic hermit. He poured some water into a small coffeepot and set the pot on top of his stove. Opening the stove door, he tossed a few small sticks of wood inside, and the flames leaped up. He closed the door again. Opening a large tin, he stuck his fist down in it and came up with a handful of coffee grounds, which he then dropped into the pot. "Won't be long," he said.

The visitor reached into a coat pocket and drew out a pipe and a pouch of tobacco. He filled the pipe bowl and put the pouch back in his pocket. Then he took out a match, reached over to the side of the wood stove, and scratched a flame out of the match. He held it to his pipe and puffed until he had the tobacco well lit. Then he sat down and puffed in silence for a moment. Then he reached back into his pocket and pulled out the pouch again, holding it out toward Billie.

"Oh," he said. "Have some?"

"No, thanks," Billie said. "Got my own."

The man put the pouch back into his pocket. He puffed some more in silence while Billie went to a shelf and got down two tin cups and put them on the table. "Coffee be ready in a minute," Billie said.

"I think it's done already," the visitor said.

"Ain't been on long enough," Billie argued.

"Check it," said the other. "I'll bet you it's done."

"I'll just show you, then," said Billie. He picked up one of the cups and walked to the stove, his back to his visitor. The man stood and quietly stepped up behind Billie. He reached with his right arm underneath the left side of his coat and withdrew a miner's hammer, raising it high over his right shoulder. Then, with a swift downward blow, he cracked open the back of Billie's skull. The only sound Billie made was a sudden exhalation. His body sagged immediately, and he fell forward, knocking over the coffeepot. As the upper portion of the limp body landed on the hot stove top and slowly slid off, the flesh on the forearms and hands and on one side of the face was burned. Then the body slumped to the floor.

Chapter Thirteen

Mitch woke up and dressed. It was early in the day, but Ellie would be opened and cooking breakfast. He walked over to the "Eat Here" tent and ordered himself some eggs and bacon. He had a leisurely breakfast, drank several cups of coffee, smoked a cigarette, and finally ordered up two meals to take over to his prisoners. Knowing that he couldn't really starve them to death, he had begun feeding them a few days earlier. The bars were supposed to be fitted to the windows in the jail on this day, and he casually wondered if the prisoners would appreciate being actually put in jail rather than being chained to its outside wall.

When Ellie brought him the two breakfasts, he touched the brim of his hat, picked them up, and walked out of the tent and back to his office. He didn't bother going into his office. He walked around on the outside. Rounding the back corner of the building, he was surprised by the sight of two lengths of chain lying in the dirt. They were still attached firmly to the log in the jail wall. The padlocks were still fastened. The prisoners were gone.

Mitch walked over to the chains and knelt there, putting the breakfasts on the ground. A hacksaw blade was lying on the ground, and Mitch could see where the chains had been cut. It would have taken some time to saw through those chains, and he reasoned that someone had given the blade to the prisoners the night before, probably not long after he had gone to bed. For a moment he wondered why the two desperadoes had not bothered trying to break into the office building to get at him, but then he thought that whoever had brought the blade had likely not brought them guns.

The office building was locked at night, too, and perhaps the two had decided that getting Mitch at that time was too big a risk. They had their freedom, and they just wanted to get the hell out of Paxton. Surely they would be back, though. Surely they would seek their revenge on the man who had killed two of their comrades, chained them up, and left them sitting on the ground hungry for a few days.

Well, they wouldn't get the chance, Mitch told himself. He would go after them. He was a tracker, a man-hunter. This was a job he felt confident with, not like trying to figure out who was bashing in the heads of unsuspecting miners. Mitch examined the ground carefully, and he found the footprints of whoever it was had tossed the two the hacksaw blade. There was something familiar about those prints. He had seen them somewhere before.

He looked further, and soon he had determined which way Dog and Hammerhead had gone. He followed their skulking tracks along the back sides of the buildings all the way down to Sam Neely's stables. There they had located their own horses, saddled them up, and ridden out of Paxton, going up the mountain. He wondered if they were stupid enough to return to the shack in which they had been living. Either that or Red's now-abandoned claim. They weren't very bright, but that would be a particularly foolish move on their part. But where else would they be headed, going up the mountain? Mitch walked around to the front of Neely's place, and when Neely saw him, he came running out of his office.

"Sheriff," he yelled. "Sheriff. Them two horses you left here—the ones that belonged to your prisoners—they're gone."

"Yeah," Mitch said. "I know."

"How'd you know?" Neely asked.

"I tracked the prisoners here," said Mitch. "Just be glad they took their own horses. Did they take anything else?"

"Just their saddles," Neely said.

"Saddle up my horse for me, will you?" said Mitch.

"You going after them?"

"That's right."

Mitch followed the tracks up to the Paxton mine and beyond. He trailed the two fugitives from there right back to their own old hangout, but they did not stop there either. They continued up the mountain, along a trail that just barely deserved the name. It was not on the map Reid had supplied him with. Mitch rode alert and with caution. Dog and Hammerhead had not taken their guns with them. Those remained locked up in Mitch's office, but they might have been able to pick some up along the way. Whoever had supplied them with the hacksaw blade might also have supplied them with weapons. He had to assume that the two were armed, and if they were armed, they would certainly be dangerous.

Mitch had ridden until well into the afternoon when he saw a shack ahead. In another minute, he saw the two horses. He recognized them as the mounts of Dog and Hammerhead. Just then a shot rang out, and Mitch felt it whiz close by his ear. He flung himself from the saddle, managing at the same time to drag his Winchester out of its sheath and take it along with him. He hit the ground rolling and pressed himself up close against the rocks that still rose high beside the trail. He could just see the shack from his new point of view. He thought that the shot had come from there.

He chambered a shell in the Winchester and took aim at the shack, but he held still, waiting. In the high mountain stillness, he could hear sudden frantic voices coming from the shack. He couldn't make out any words, but he thought that he could recognize the voices of Dog and Hammerhead arguing in their desperation. He thought that he'd increase their anxiety a bit, and he fired a shot into the shack. He pressed himself hard into the rocks as a barrage of shots followed, some of them coming close enough to kick dust or flecks of rock into his shoulder and head.

From the reports, he decided that the two rats in the shack had only handguns. That was a relief, and it explained why the shots were mostly wide. It also meant that the shooters would have to reload after six shots each, and then Mitch wondered if the two men had a good supply of shells or not. How long would they be able to hold out inside the shack? The frantic firing from the shack came to a stop as suddenly as it had started. There were no voices, either. Mitch figured the two were reloading.

"Dog," he shouted. "Hammerhead. That you in the shack?"

"It's us, all right, you son of a bitch," one of them answered. Mitch thought that it was Dog.

"Toss out your guns," Mitch called out.

"Fat chance, Injun," Hammerhead yelled.

"I don't want to have to kill you boys," Mitch said. "All I want is to take you back to jail. Right now all you're charged with is assaulting an officer of the Don't make it more serious. Throw out your guns."

There was a new barrage of fire from the shack, and Mitch waited it out as before. When it stopped, as before, Mitch yelled again toward the shack.

"How many shells you boys got in there?" he said. There was no answer. "You're going to run out sooner or later," he added. "Then I'll get you."

"We got plenty," Dog hollered. "Don't you worry none about that. You worry about your own self. It's going to get dark after a spell, and it's going to get cold. How're you set up out there? Huh? Think about that."

If the two did have plenty of bullets, as Dog claimed, then the possibility of their holding out until nightfall was something to think about. There was already a chill in the air, and Mitch could tell that it would be a cold night. His blanket was tied on behind his saddle. Of course, if the standoff lasted until dark, he could probably get to his horse without too much trouble. He didn't want it to last that long, however. He tried to think of some way to bring things to a head. Suddenly there were more shots, and Mitch's horse panicked. It neighed and stamped its feet. The trail was narrow, so it was frustrated in its attempt to turn and run. Finally it ran blindly ahead and wound up bumping into the horses of the two fugitives. Eventually it settled down again, apparently comforted somewhat by the close company of two of its own kind. So much for getting to his blanket if he should need it, Mitch thought.

He fired another round into the shack, and it had its desired effect, causing another barrage. Maybe he could force the two fools inside to use up all their ammunition. The problem with that was that one of the two might get off a lucky shot and actually hit him. But so far, Mitch's luck had held. Mitch looked over to the other side of the trail. It dropped off, but he couldn't tell how sharp a drop it was. The incline was covered with a thick growth of scrubby trees and brush. It looked like, if he could get himself over there, he might be able to work himself closer to the shack. That is, if he could get over there and off the trail without falling, and if, once there, he could work his way through that growth.

It would be taking a chance, but at the same time it would cause something to happen. Mitch had the patience to wait it out, if he needed to do that. He also figured that he could stand the cold more than most, if he had to. But he didn't have to. He decided to try it. He studied the layout across the trail and picked his spot. Then he raised himself up onto his feet, staying in a low crouch, and took a dive for the other side. Shots rang out as Mitch threw himself into the brush. He grabbed desperately for branches as he felt himself falling, but he didn't fall for long. The thickness of the growth inhibited his fall. He looked over his shoulder, but he still couldn't tell much about the steepness of the incline or the distance to the bottom. The brush was just too thick. He settled himself as best he could on the slanted ground. The firing from the shack had stopped again.

He inched himself up for a better look, then saw that Hammerhead had come out of the shack and was running in his direction. Mitch struggled to get set in a position from which he could fire the rifle, but branches were in his way. He dropped it and pulled out his Colt, raising it up to firing position as Hammerhead started shooting his own revolver. Mitch squeezed off a round, and Hammerhead jerked but kept running. Mitch fired again, his second slug striking Hammerhead in the heart. Hammerhead ran two more long strides, his arms flapping wildly, his head bouncing loosely on his shoulders. Then he pitched forward, plowing his face into the hard ground.

Then Dog ran out and over to the horses. He was trying to settle a horse and climb into the saddle, but the horse was skittish. Dog was hopping around, trying to get a foot into a stirrup. He had both hands on the saddle horn, but his revolver was still in his right hand. Mitch climbed back up onto the narrow trail.

"Dog," he shouted. "Hold it."

Dog turned loose of the horse and turned to face Mitch. He fired a wild shot, and Mitch leveled his Colt. Dog fired another shot that went wide, and Mitch pulled the trigger. His lead smashed into Dog's forehead, and Mitch grumbled. He had aimed lower. Dog's head wobbled back and forth as his knees slowly buckled. Then his body crumpled into a wad on the ground. Mitch holstered his Colt, then turned to look for his Winchester. Luckily it had hung up in brush. He went back down the edge far enough to retrieve it.

Climbing back up on the trail, Mitch checked the two bodies. Both were dead. He had known they were. He loaded Dog onto a horse, then walked back over to the body of Hammerhead. He dragged it to the horses and loaded it. He thought about mounting up to ride back to Paxton, but his curiosity got the better of him. This shack had not been on the map that Reid had provided him with. He decided to check it out.

He went inside, and there on the floor was a body, its head bashed in from behind.

Chapter Fourteen

It was the next morning when Mitch rode back into Paxton with his grim load, and he rode straight to the office of J. Paxton Reid. He saw right away that the office was still locked, so he sat in the saddle and waited. In a few minutes, Reid came walking up to his office door. Seeing Mitch, and the bodies draped over the two extra horses, he stopped, stared a moment, then walked over to Mitch.

"I see you got them," he said. "Who's the third one? The one who helped them escape?"

"I don't know who helped them escape," said Mitch. "As for that extra body, I wish you'd tell me."

Reid gave Mitch a look, then walked over to the horse carrying the one body. He started to grab it by the hair to raise the head, but he hesitated. The back of the head was matted with blood. Reid could see right away that it was another victim of the mysterious head-basher. He leaned over, then knelt to get a look at the face without having to touch the head. Then he straightened up.

"It's old Billie Whitehead," he said.

"I found him in a mining shack," said Mitch. "It wasn't on my map."

"Hell," said Reid, "I didn't think about him. He's so far out—he *was* so far out—that I never even thought of him as part of this community. How'd you happen to be way out there?"

"I followed these two out there," said Mitch. "After I killed them I took a look inside the shack and found him."

"I guess that clears it all up," Reid said.

"It don't clear up nothing," said Mitch. "These two never killed him."

"What makes you say that?" Reid asked, but noticing that people were starting to gather on the board sidewalk, he added quickly. "Never mind. Go on in my office and wait for me. I'll get these bodies taken off the street." He dug a key out of his pocket and handed it to Mitch, who dismounted, unlocked the door, and went inside. He walked on back to the private office and took a seat. Then he rolled himself a smoke and lit it. He had just finished it when Reid came in.

"All right," Reid said, moving to the chair behind his desk, "what makes you say those two didn't kill old Billie? You found them there at his place and found him dead inside."

"In the first place," Mitch answered, "I figure the same man who killed the others killed Whitehead, and I never thought them two and their two partners had anything to do with any of them. Besides that, I think that Whitehead was dead when Dog and Hammerhead got there. There wasn't none of his blood on either one of them, and there wasn't no bloody blunt weapon around nowhere."

"That's it?" Reid asked.

"I seen some tracks up there," said Mitch. "They looked like some tracks I found out by the jail. It looks like to me that the killer turned them two loose. Maybe to just take my attention away from him for a while. By the way, I seen them same tracks, I'm sure, up at Big Bob's shack, up there where Orr was killed.''

"So all you have to do is find the man whose boots match those tracks," Reid said.

"That could take a long time," said Mitch. "I need to find a way of smoking the man out."

"What do you mean?" Reid asked.

"Make him come to me," said Mitch. "It'd be a lot faster."

"And just how do you propose to do that?"

"I ain't figured that out yet."

Reid took a cigar out of the box on top of his desk. "By the way," he said, "you still have my name on that list of suspects?" He struck a match and touched it to the end of the cigar.

"I ain't took any names off the list yet," said Mitch.

"Then do me a favor," Reid said. "Add your own name to the list. After all, you put Manny on there just because he found Orr's body. Now you've found two of them yourself."

"The first two killings took place before I even got here," Mitch said.

Just then the front door opened and closed again, and following footsteps across the front office, there was a polite rap on the door. Mitch looked over his shoulder as Reid said, "What can I do for you?" A smooth-faced man of medium height was standing with a bowler in his hand.

"Are you Mr. Reid," the man asked, "the mayor?"

"I'm Reid."

The man looked at Mitch then. "I could come back later," he said. "I didn't mean to interrupt anything."

"We're done," Mitch said, standing up. "Come on in."

The man moved in a few steps. "I'm Harvey Radin," he said. "I'm a newspaperman, and I have my own press. I heard about your town, and I also heard that you have no paper here. Is that correct?"

"That's correct," said Reid. "We're a new town."

"I'd like to set up shop here," said Radin.

"I just happen to know a building that would be perfect

for you," Reid said, a smile spreading across his face. He stood up and rounded the desk to pump Radin's hand. "Where's your equipment?"

"It's right outside," Radin said. "In my wagon."

"Come on," Reid said. "I'll show you the building."

Reid rushed Radin back outside, sweeping past Mitch without another word. Mitch casually followed them out. If there was going to be a newspaper in Paxton, he thought that he ought to know where it would be. He followed Reid and Radin to an empty building next door to the general store.

"Old Dick Porter was going to open up a butcher shop," Reid explained in anticipation of the obvious question, "but he died before he got around to it. That's why we happen to have an empty building in a boomtown like this. Anyhow, I can let you have it for the newspaper."

Mitch decided that he'd seen enough. He wasn't interested in the details of how Reid would transfer the building or the use of it to Radin. He'd only wanted to know where the paper would be. He turned to leave, but Reid, suddenly aware of him again, stopped him. "Hold up, Mitch," he said. Mitch paused. "Mr. Radin," Reid said, "this is our sheriff, Mitch Frye."

Mitch and Radin shook hands, and Mitch excused himself. He walked to Ellie's for some coffee. It had been a long night and day, and he needed some sleep, but he wanted coffee first. He found Jewel sitting alone under the big tent, and he walked over to join her. "You mind?" he said.

"Of course not," she said.

Mitch sat across from her, feeling good in the knowledge that he was doing something that Reid had forbade. "I guess I look some rugged," he said. "I been out all night."

"Want to tell me about it?" Jewel asked.

Mitch shrugged. "My prisoners broke out," he said.

"I heard," she said. "So you went after them?"

"Yeah."

"Did you bring them back?" she asked him.

"Yeah."

"Dead or alive?"

"They didn't give me no choice," Mitch said. "I killed them."

"Somehow that doesn't surprise me," Jewel said.

"I'll sit somewhere else," said Mitch, rising halfway up from the bench. Jewel reached across the table and stopped him with a hand on his arm.

"Sit down," she said. "I'm sorry. I didn't mean that. Well, I didn't mean it that way."

Mitch settled back down on the bench. "I'm just touchy, I guess," he said. "I found another dead miner out there."

"Oh, no," Jewel said. "Who was he?"

"Your old man identified him for me," Mitch said. "Billie Whitehead."

"My God," said Jewel. "Way out there."

Ellie came over, and Mitch ordered his coffee. When Ellie left their table, he said, "I followed Dog and Hammerhead out there. Otherwise it might have been a long time before anyone come across the body."

"But why—"

"I still think they all had something in common," Mitch said. "If only I could find out what it was."

"What's your next step?" Jewel asked.

"I don't know," Mitch said. "Like I told your old man, I need to come up with some way of making him come to me. I just ain't thought of a way to do that." Ellie brought the coffee, and Mitch thanked her. She hustled off again. "We're getting a newspaper," he said. "Did you know that?"

"No," she said. "Who's—"

"Fellow named Radin," said Mitch. "He just rolled into town. Your old man took him over to show him the place next door to the general store."

"That's great," she said. "I can hardly wait for the first issue."

"He just got in town," Mitch said. "I reckon he won't have much to write about yet."

"I guess not," she said. "Unless . . ."

"What?" said Mitch.

"Unless you give him something," she said, suddenly excited. She looked around to see how close to them any other customers were sitting. "Finish your coffee," she said, "and let's go over to your office. I've got an idea."

In the office Mitch sat in his chair and Jewel sat on the edge of the desk. Her excitement had not abated any.

"What did you say your next move should be?" she asked.

"I don't recall just what I said," Mitch answered. "But what I need to do is I need to smoke out the killer."

"All right," said Jewel. "Here's a way. You said you think the killings are all related. That the victims all had something in common. Right?"

"That's right," Mitch said.

"Well," Jewel continued, "if the murderer's not done yet, if he's still got anyone left on his list, then I think I know a way to get someone to come forward."

"I'm listening," Mitch said.

"Suppose you give Radin his first big story," she said. "Suppose the newspaper says that someone's killing miners around here, and that there's a connection between all the murders. If the connection is a real one and there's anyone left who might be the next victim, the story might scare him into coming to you for help."

"It might, and it might not," Mitch said, "but it's sure worth a try."

He stood up and put his hat back on his head.

"Where're you going?" Jewel asked.

"To see Radin."

"I'm going with you," she said, and she hurried along behind him as he left the office.

103

Chapter Fifteen

The first edition of *The Paxton Gazette* carried the following headline:

MYSTERIOUS MURDERS RELATED, SAYS SHERIFF

Beneath the bold headline, half of the front page was taken up with the following story:

Four miners have been murdered in the vicinity of Paxton in the last few weeks. Each victim was discovered with his head bashed in from behind. According to Sheriff Mitch Frye, robbery was a possible motive in only one of the cases, that of Howard Jones, an employee of the Paxton Mine.

The body of Jones was discovered in the Paxton mine's office, and one hundred thousand dollars in cash, the payroll money for the mine, was missing. Also missing was another Paxton employee, Marvin Duncklee.

Duncklee was pursued by Paxton's new sheriff, Mitch Frye. Frye killed Duncklee and recovered the payroll. The case was thought to be closed.

Then Manny Gordon discovered the body of miner George Orr in Orr's own mine shack. Like Jones's, Orr's head had been bashed in. Within a week's time, the bodies of Red Calhoun and Billie Whitehead were found, both killed in the same manner as the others.

Sheriff Frye believes that the same killer is responsible for all four murders, and that Duncklee was simply a goat. There are no suspects. The only evidence in the case is a distinctive footprint.

Immediately below that article and to the left of the page was a shorter one with the following headline: WHO WILL BE NEXT? The story read as follows:

Paxton's sheriff, Mitch Frye, believes that the four recent murder victims all had something in common. If that something could be discovered, he says, he would find the killer. He says further that he fears there may yet be someone else out there, another miner perhaps, who shared with the victims that commonality. If so, he says, that someone will likely be the killer's next victim.

Mitch was sitting behind his desk studying the growing list and notes he continued to make on the case of the murdered miners when Jewel Reid came bursting into the room with the first copy of the new *Gazette*. She flung it on the desk in front of him.

"Here it is," she said. "You think that will smoke him out?"

She perched on the edge of Mitch's desk while he read the two front-page stories. Mitch rolled himself a smoke while he was reading. Jewel fidgeted, anxious for Mitch to finish so she could get his reaction. When it came, she was a little disappointed. He lit his cigarette and leaned back in his chair.

"It might work," he said. "I wonder if I made a mistake giving Radin that bit about the footprint."

"Why would it be a mistake?" Jewel asked.

"If the man reads the story," Mitch said, "he'll likely just throw away them boots."

"Well," she said, "who cares? You're not going to be wandering around looking at footprints anyhow. You're going to wait for him to show himself. You're smoking him out, remember?"

"Yeah," said Mitch. "I hope it works."

"I'm confident that it will," Jewel said. "There's another story inside that might interest you."

She leaned over and turned the page, indicating with a finger the story she had made reference to. It was titled, "Paxton's New Sheriff," and the story under the heading read as follows:

Paxton is indeed fortunate to have as its first sheriff Mr. Mitch Frye, formerly a scout for the United States Army. Frye was active in pursuit of the notorious Apache Geronimo, while under the command of General George Crook. He worked alongside the great scout Al Sieber and another well-known frontiersman, Tom Horn. We are blessed to have such an experienced manhunter as Mitch Frye working for the good of our community.

Mitch gave a grunt and folded the paper back to the front page.

"It's a nice story," Jewel said. "Don't you agree?"

"I guess," Mitch said.

"Have you had your breakfast?" Jewel asked him.

"No."

"Let's go to over to the best restaurant in town," she said.

"You mean Ellie's tent?" he said.

"That's the place."

*   *   *

106

When they walked into Ellie's, the first person they saw was Jasper Boone. He was sitting by himself, just finishing his meal. "Good morning," he said.

"Howdy, Boone," Mitch said.

"Good morning, Jasper," said Jewel.

"Join me?" Boone offered.

They sat down at the table with Boone, and soon had placed their orders with Ellie.

"I just read the morning paper," Boone said. "First edition. It's about time we had a newspaper in this town. Have you met the editor yet?"

"Mr. Radin," said Jewel. "He seems like a nice man."

"He did a good story on you, Sheriff," Boone said. "Brief but to the point. I agree with what he said, too."

"Thanks," Mitch said. "It wasn't needed."

"Oh, well," Boone said, "you might be pleased to know, then, that we'll finish up the jail today. We got the bars installed yesterday. All we have to do now is hang the main door and install the locks. We'll be done by lunchtime."

"That's good," said Mitch.

Ellie brought Mitch's and Jewel's meals, and Boone, having finished his, excused himself and left the tent.

"Now you'll have a place to lock up prisoners," Jewel said. "Paxton's starting to look like a real town. All we need is a church and a school."

Mitch couldn't really see a reason for either one of those, but he kept his opinion to himself and started eating his breakfast. He was surprised to find himself thinking about his new jail—"his," he had called it in his thoughts. He had not given it much consideration before, but now that it was almost finished, he had developed a sudden interest. He was anxious to see it. He was even, he thought with a silent chuckle, anxious to arrest someone and make use of the new facility.

He finished eating well before Jewel, so he had some more coffee. He was impatient for her to finish. He wanted to go look at the jail, but he didn't want to walk out and leave Jewel alone. It wouldn't seem right. He drank his coffee and waited for her. When at last she had done, he stood up.

"Want to go check out the new jail with me?" he asked her.

"Sure," she said.

They walked to his office and around the outside of the building to the new jail in back. As soon as they rounded the corner, Mitch stopped to study the outside of the jail. Funny, he thought, that he had never really looked at it before. It appeared to be a solid log structure. The windows were barred. He walked over to the nearest window and took hold of two bars, giving them a hard tug. They were set in solidly. He walked to the front entranceway, where Boone and another workman were preparing to hang the door.

"Can we go inside?" Mitch asked.

"Sure," said Boone.

It was then that he noticed the footprint just outside the new jail. It was the same as the ones he had seen that belonged to the man who had given a hacksaw blade to his prisoners, the same one he had seen at the shack of Big Bob and George Orr. It was the footprint, he believed, of the killer, and it was not where the others had been, not where the man had made his approach to rescue the prisoners. It was there with the footprints of the workmen. Not wanting to alert anyone, Mitch kept quiet. He walked on through the door to examine the jail's interior. Jewel followed him.

There was a hallway straight through the center of the building and leading to a back door. On either side of the hallway were cells, two on each side. Mitch checked one of the heavy wooden doors with small barred windows. The locks had not yet been installed. That was part of the finishing work Boone had made reference to. He opened one of the cell doors to look inside. The cell had a barred window, a cot against one wall, and a small table and straight-backed chair. Nothing more. He went back out to the central hallway and walked to the back door. Like the other doors, it was waiting for its lock.

He opened the door and stepped outside. There were many footprints out there, and among them he saw again the one print in which he was interested. It belonged to one of the workmen, he told himself. It had to. He decided to hang around, as if he were involved in the finishing up of the jail, and watch to see what kind of print each of the men left. In a few minutes Jewel made her excuses and left. Mitch stayed. He made small talk with the different men working on the job. There were four of them altogether, counting Jasper Boone.

Boone's prediction proved true. By noon the work was all done, but more important, Mitch had seen the mark left by each of the four men on the ground. He was frustrated. None of them matched the telltale print he had identified as belonging to the murderer. He considered having a talk with Jasper Boone, but then he told himself that no matter how much he liked the man, he was, technically, one of the four new suspects. He decided to pay a visit to Reid.

"Let's go see Mr. Reid," Boone said just then to the other three workmen. "We'll tell him we're finished and collect our pay."

"I'm all for that," said one of the men.

"Me too," said another. "I want to get good and drunk."

"If you don't mind," Mitch said, "I'll walk along with you."

"That's good," Boone said. "You can tell Mr. Reid that you've examined the work."

They found Reid in his office, and with Mitch's assurance that the work was done and done well, Reid paid Boone. Boone then counted out money for each of the other three, thanked Reid, and the four workmen left the office. Mitch stayed. Reid looked up at him from behind the big desk.

"Something else?" he asked.

"I want you to tell me everything you know about each of those four men," Mitch said.

"What for?" said Reid.

"You know that footprint I've been looking for?" Mitch asked. "It's mixed in with theirs all around the jail."

"You mean you now suspect one of those four men?" Reid said.

"That's right," Mitch said, "and whichever one it is, he's gone right to the top of the list."

"Well, did you check their footprints?"

"Sure, but he's changed his boots," Mitch said. "It has to be one of them, though. The print's all over the place out there."

"You're assuming a lot about that footprint, aren't you, Mitch?" said Reid.

"It was the only unidentified print out at the site of Orr's murder," Mitch said, "and I know that it belongs to the man who helped Dog and Hammerhead escape. If there's anything I know about, it's reading sign. Now I know that it was also made by one of those four men."

Reid heaved a sigh. "All right," he said. "The contractor's name is Jasper Boone. He's a carpenter by trade. Came here like everyone else, looking for gold, but he decided he'd do better by following his rightful trade. He's done all right. A new town needs builders."

"I've met Boone," Mitch said. "How long's he been around?"

"Oh, he came to town a couple of months ago, I'd say."

"He didn't hunt gold very long," Mitch said.

"Early on," Reid said, "I'd agree with you, but now it doesn't take long at all to find out that all the decent claims have already been staked out."

"What else do you know about him?"

"Nothing. It's like we've said before, Mitch. When a man rides into Paxton, no one asks questions about his past."

"Who're the others?" Mitch asked.

"There's Ollie Burns, Melvin Tucker, and, uh, Hiram Hubert," Reid said. "And I know less about them than I do about Boone. Sorry."

"Do you know where they live?" Mitch asked.

"I'll draw you another map," said Reid.

Chapter Sixteen

Jasper Boone had a room in Paxton's only hotel. Burns and
Tucker lived in a small shack at the edge of town, and Hubert
had pitched himself a small canvas tent at the lower end of
town. As inconspicuously as he could, Mitch wandered
around all the residences. He found no more of the footprints
for which he searched. Finally he went to the town dump
down the side of the mountain behind the town. There he
found the boots. He took them back to his office and put
them in a bottom desk drawer. He assumed that the killer
had, indeed, read the paper.

He decided that he would have to be more direct. He
would interview all four carpenters. He found Ollie Burns at
Ellie's drinking coffee. He told Ellie to put the coffee on his
tab, which, of course, Reid would pay in the name of the
town, and he asked Burns to walk over to the sheriff's office
with him.

"What's it all about, Sheriff?" Burns said.

"I just want to have a talk with you," Mitch said. "Come on."

Burns followed Mitch to the office. Mitch gestured toward the straight chair by the desk, and Burns sat down. He was nervous, Mitch could tell that. Mitch went around to the other side of the desk and sat down. He pulled open the bottom drawer, took out the boots, and dropped them heavily on top of the desk. He looked at Burns. Burns seemed perplexed.

"I found these in the dump," Mitch said.

He waited for any telltale reaction from Burns, but all he got was a continued look of perplexity. After a long moment of silence, Burns shrugged. "So," he said, "what am I supposed to say? What do you want from me?"

"Have you ever seen those boots before?" Mitch asked.

"Boots is boots," Burns said. "I don't go around looking at boots."

"Are they yours?"

"They ain't mine," Burns said. "No. I got one pair, and I'm wearing them."

"Could they belong to Tucker or Hubert?" Mitch asked. "Or Boone?"

"How would I know?" said Burns. "Like I said, I don't go around looking at boots. Oh. They ain't Tucker's."

"How do you know that?" Mitch asked.

"Tucker wears shoes," said Burns. "Always shoes. I never seen him in boots."

"I thought you said you never look at boots," Mitch said.

"I don't, but—Well, I mean, I guess I notice sometimes if a man is wearing boots or shoes, but I don't go studying on his boots. I could have seen them boots before, but I don't know. What's this all about? You trying to trap me into something? What is it with those boots, anyhow?"

"Never mind, Burns," Mitch said. "I just wanted to find out if you'd recognize those boots. Thanks for coming over. That's all."

* * *

112

Mitch interviewed Tucker and Hubert with much the same results. He decided it was time to have a visit with Boone. He liked Boone, and he didn't want to think that Boone might be the killer. He told himself, rather, that he might take Boone into his confidence. If the boots did really belong to one of the other three men, perhaps Boone would be able to help. He was unable to find Boone that day, so he thought that he'd try to catch him at Ellie's the next morning. It had been a long day, and an even longer and frustrating case. He suddenly decided to have himself a drink, so he walked over to the Golden Monkey.

The tent saloon was crowded and busy. It was almost too noisy for the bartender to hear Mitch's order, but he managed to get himself a shot of whiskey. With the drink on the bar in front of him, he thought about Al and Tom. Most of his drinking had been done with those two veteran scouts. He wished that he was with them yet, and he wondered if he had made a big mistake in not going along with them to Tucson.

Al and Tom were the only two friends he had, and he had parted company with them. And for what? He had wandered into Paxton and got himself caught in Reid's trap. He was the sheriff, and he had a fat bankroll, more money than he had ever had at one time in his life, but even so, he was virtually a prisoner of Reid. A prisoner in Paxton—Reid's town. He wondered what Al Sieber would do in a situation like this, but then he told himself Al would never have fallen into such a trap.

He downed the whiskey and ordered himself another. With two or three shots, he'd get a good night's sleep. He thought about the old days of chasing Geronimo and his followers through the mountains and even down into old Mexico with Al and Tom, and he longed for that freedom once again, the freedom of the vast spaces, the fresh air, the silence of the land away from busy towns and the comfort of knowing his enemy, the confidence of knowing his job and knowing that he was good at it.

He found his predicament not unbearable, but at least distasteful. Not only had the job been forced on him, not only was he being, in effect, held against his will, but the job itself was one he would never have chosen for himself. He had never even liked lawmen. He had never been in trouble with the law, but he had always found lawmen to be bullies or at least pompous bastards who tried to lord it over everyone. While he had been wandering alone away from Al and Tom, and wondering what he could do with himself since the Army had dismissed him, he had considered bounty hunting, but it had been low on his list. Even bounty hunting, he now told himself, would be preferable to this sheriff's job.

He finished his drink and ordered a third shot. Goddamn J. Paxton Reid and his town of Paxton and his Paxton mine, he told himself. He wanted to shout the words out loud, but he knew that it would do no good. He thought he'd like to push Reid's face in and burn the town clear off the map. But of course he would not. He'd put up with his situation, as unpleasant as it was, for a while longer, long enough to figure a way out of it.

First he had to find the killer of the miners. But why? he asked himself. Why did he have to find the killer? Suppose he never found the killer. So what? What would Reid do about it? Fire him? It seemed to Mitch that the best thing he could do was show himself to be incompetent. Then perhaps Reid would fire him and set him free. It seemed the best thing, yet he knew that he would not be able to play it that way. He wanted to find the killer. He wanted to stop the man, but most of all, he admitted to himself, he wanted to prove that he could do it. He didn't want to be outsmarted by a man like—Well, he didn't want the Paxton head-basher to get the best of him. That was all.

He ordered another drink, and when he had sipped it halfway down, he began to feel a bit woozy. He wasn't used to that much alcohol. The times he had gone drinking with Al and Tom, he had passed out before either of those two. He called for a water chaser and ordered another shot of whiskey at the same time. All of a sudden he realized that his intention was to get drunk. He finished the shot on the bar in front of him, and the bartender brought the next one along with a glass of water.

Mitch felt like he was beginning to weave ever so slightly, and it was beginning to be difficult to focus his eyes on anything. He didn't want to make a fool of himself in public, so he finished his last shot and turned away from the bar. Holding himself straight and taking a deep breath, he started toward the front door. He could tell that he was not walking straight, that if anyone was bothering to watch him, they could tell that he'd had too much. He felt as if all eyes in the Monkey were on him as he made his way through the crowd.

He was relieved to be outside, but there were still people walking up and down the board sidewalks. Heading for his office, he stayed close to the wall. Someone spoke to him, and he mumbled a reply. He didn't notice who it had been. He staggered a few steps, and then he knew that he was about to fall. He pressed himself against the wall and let himself down to the walk. Then he went to sleep and fell over on his side.

Mitch felt himself being roused out of a deep sleep by someone shaking him roughly. He heard a voice that seemed to be coming at him through a tunnel. He tried to open his eyes, but the lids were heavy. He did manage to roll over and moan, and then he opened one eye, and he saw Jasper Boone kneeling there beside him.

"Jasper?" he said.

"Mitch," said Boone, "get up. Come on. I'll help you. We've got to get you out of the street." Mitch got to his feet with Boone's help, and Boone threw Mitch's arm around his shoulder. "Come on," he said. "Come on. You're not going to be sick, are you?"

"I ain't going to puke, if that's what you're worried about," Mitch mumbled.

"Well," said Boone, "here we are. You have a door key?"

Mitch fumbled in his pocket for the key. Pulling it out, he

dropped it. Boone leaned him against the wall and picked up the key. He unlocked the door, put the key back in Mitch's pocket, and took Mitch inside and back to his bed in the back room. As Mitch stretched out, Boone said, "I can't lock the door for you when I leave."

"That's all right," Mitch said. "I'll get up in a few minutes and lock it."

"You sure?" Boone asked.

"It's all right," Mitch said, waving an arm. "Go on. I'm all right."

"Well, all right," said Boone. "I'll see you tomorrow."

"Yeah," said Mitch. "Hey, Jasper. Thanks."

"Forget it," Boone said, and he headed for the door.

"Wait a minute," Mitch said.

"Yeah?"

"In the morning," said Mitch, his voice still slurred, "stop by and get me for breakfast."

Chapter Seventeen

When Jasper Boone stopped by the sheriff's office the next morning, he found the front door unlocked. He walked in, but Mitch was not at his desk. He was nowhere to be seen. Boone called out to him: "Mitch." He received no answer. He walked to the back room and opened the door. Mitch was still in his bed. Boone called out again: "Mitch." Mitch stirred a bit. "Wake up, Mitch," Boone said. Mitch lifted his head and opened his eyes, slowly focusing on Boone there at the door. "The last thing you said when I left you was to call on you for breakfast," Boone explained.

"Oh," said Mitch, rubbing his face. "Oh, yeah. It's that time already, is it?"

"It's that time," Boone responded.

"Well, give me a couple of minutes to get dressed," Mitch said.

"I'll have a seat out in your office," said Boone, and he stepped out, closing the door.

Boone didn't have to wait long. In a few minutes, Mitch

117

appeared wearing clean clothes and looking fresh. "Ready to go?" Boone asked.

"In a minute," Mitch said. "I want to show you something first."

As Mitch moved behind his desk, Boone said, "I found the door unlocked. You didn't get up and lock it after I left, did you?"

"I guess not," said Mitch. "I kind of tied one on last night. I appreciate you picking me up and bringing me home."

"Ah, forget it," Boone said. "But you should have locked your door."

"Yeah," Mitch agreed. "Don't worry. I don't do that but once a year."

He pulled the boots out of the bottom desk drawer.

"When the next time comes around," said Boone, "let me know ahead of time. I'll be sure you get home all right, and I'll be sure you lock your door."

Mitch dropped the boots on the desktop.

"You ever see these before?" he asked.

Boone scrutinized the boots. He picked them up for a better look.

"Can't say for sure," he said. "They're a pretty common kind of boot. Look to be about my size."

He crossed one leg over the other and held the sole of one of the boots against the sole of his own.

"Try it on," Mitch said.

Boone gave him a curious look, shrugged, then pulled a boot off his foot. He pulled the evidence boot on and stood up. "Well," he said, "I was close, but it kind of pinches." He sat back down to remove the boot and replace his own. "What's this all about, Mitch?"

Mitch put the boots back in the desk drawer and stood up. "Come on," he said. "I'll tell you over breakfast. I need some coffee real bad."

They walked to Ellie's place in silence, went inside, and ordered their breakfasts. Ellie brought them coffee right away. The hot coffee was a relief to Mitch. He had a slight headache from the night before.

"All right, Sheriff," Boone said, "what's the mystery?"

"Jasper," said Mitch, "when I went up to Big Bob's shack to check out the scene of George Orr's killing, I found one set of prints that I couldn't identify. I memorized them. I seen them again the morning my two prisoners escaped. From the way the tracks lay, I figured out that the man who left them had slipped up and tossed those two boys a hacksaw blade."

"They matched the prints you'd seen at George and Bob's place?" Boone asked.

"That's right," said Mitch. "And that ain't all." Boone waited while Mitch sipped his coffee. "When I went out to the jail while you were hanging the door," Mitch continued, "I walked around closer than I had before, and I seen them there too. I figured then that they had to belong to one of . . . well, to one of you four builders. I checked with the others yesterday. Couldn't find you. They all said the boots wasn't theirs and they'd never seen them before."

"I see," Boone said. "And now I've said the same thing. So it looks to you like one of us is lying, and it also looks to you like one of us is the killer."

Mitch sipped some more coffee. "That's one way of looking at it," he said.

"Is that how you're looking at it?" Boone asked.

"Jasper," said Mitch, "I'm just checking out every angle. I'm looking at everything I can find. Whoever owned those boots threw them away after the story came out in the paper. They look to me to have some good use left in them."

Just then Ellie returned with the meals, and the conversation came to a halt. They ate in near silence, and when Boone had finished and pushed his plate back, he sat up straight, took a sip of coffee, then said, "Well, Mitch, are you going to arrest me?"

Mitch looked up. "What for?" he asked.

"For all those murders," said Boone.

"All four of you builders have exactly the same evidence

119

against you,'' said Mitch. ''And even if I could pin it down to just one of you, it ain't much. It ain't enough to hang a man with.''

''What would you say the murder weapon was?'' Boone asked.

''I'd say it was a hammer of some kind,'' Mitch said.

''That points at a carpenter,'' said Boone. ''And you said that the man who belongs to those boots tossed your two prisoners a hacksaw blade. A carpenter again.''

''Maybe so, Jasper, but anyone can own a hammer and a hacksaw.''

Ellie came around to pour more coffee, and the conversation stopped again until she had gone on. Just then Jewel walked in. Mitch, anxious in a way to put an end to the discussion with Boone, waved her over to their table.

''Good morning, gentlemen,'' she said, sitting down beside Boone to face Mitch across the table. ''You're just about finished.''

''I've got some more coffee drinking to do,'' Mitch said.

''You know,'' said Boone, ''there was a number of old boys from around town who stopped by while we were building the jail. Just hanging around to watch the progress. Any one of them might have left those boot prints.''

Mitch pondered that statement for a moment. ''Thanks,'' he said. In a way he was relieved, for he really didn't want Jasper Boone to be high on his list of suspects, but in another way he found that new bit of information frustrating, for it meant that he was almost back where he had started. The killer could be anyone in town, anyone who had happened by the building site. ''Do you recall who they were?'' he asked.

''I could come up with some names,'' said Boone. ''The other guys could help.''

''We'll do that,'' Mitch said. ''Could you round up your crew again and bring them by the office sometime today?''

''I'll do it,'' Boone said.

''What are you two talking about?'' Jewel asked.

''Boot prints,'' said Boone.

Ellie came to take Jewel's order then. While she was at it, she refilled Mitch's coffee cup. Boone declined, made his excuses, and left Mitch and Jewel alone.

"What about the boot prints?" Jewel asked Mitch.

"I found the same prints all around the jail," Mitch told her, "and I went to the dump and found the boots. I thought that Jasper or one of his crew must be the man I'm looking for, but Jasper just told me they had a lot of curious visitors around the building site while they was working, so I'm right back where I started."

"I see," Jewel said. She sipped some coffee, then put the cup down. "You know, there's talk going around town about you."

"What kind of talk?" he asked her.

"About last night," she said. "About . . ."

"How I got drunk and fell down in the street?" he said.

"Um-hmm."

"Well, if anyone else says anything to you about it," he said, "tell them that I said I'll do it all over again in about a year. If I'm still in Paxton, they can watch."

Jewel giggled. "All right," she said. "I'll tell them."

"Your old man say anything?" he asked.

"No," she said. "He didn't."

"That's too bad," said Mitch. "I was hoping he might fire me for it."

"He'd come closer to firing you for sitting here with me like this," she said. "Is that why you're keeping me company?"

"It's part of the reason," he said. "It was the main reason at first. Just to goad him a little, I guess."

"Now?" she said.

Mitch shrugged. "You and Jasper are the only two people in this damn town I can talk to," he said.

"Well," Jewel said, "I guess that will have to do."

Early in the afternoon, Jasper Boone showed up in Mitch's office with Tucker, Hubert, and Burns in tow. "Well, here we are," he said.

121

Mitch stood up.

"Thanks for coming in," he said. "All of you. Sit down."
Mitch reached into the desk drawer for the now-notorious
boots and put them back on top of the desk. "You all remember these, I'm sure," he said. Jasper just told me that
while you were building the jail, you had a number of visitors—curious folks wanting to see the new jail going up, I
guess. What I want you to do is try to recall as many of their
names as you can. Make me out a list."

He took paper and pencil out of a desk drawer and laid
them in front of Boone.

"You're looking for the man who fits them boots?" Burns
asked.

"That's right," Mitch said. "Whoever it was left prints
around the jail."

"Old Lang hung around quite a bit," Burns said. "Seems
like he come around most every day."

"That's right," Tucker agreed. "Son of a bitch was always trying to tell us how to do our work."

Boone wrote down the name of Andy Lang. "Old High
Pockets," he said, and he wrote that name down underneath
the first one.

"Beaver Smith," Hubert added, and Boone wrote again.

In a short while, Boone presented Mitch with a list of a
dozen names. "Can't think of any others," he said, "but all
of these were around some. Some more than others. The ones
that spent the most time with us are at the top of the list."

"Thanks, men," said Mitch, looking over the names.
"Jasper, can you hang around a bit?"

"Sure," said Boone.

The others all left the office, and then Mitch said, "You
got some more time this afternoon?"

"All you want," said Boone.

"I'd like to kind of wander around town," Mitch said.
"See how many of these men you can point out to me—
without letting on to them."

"You ready now?" Boone asked him.

"Let's go," said Mitch.

They went into Ellie's first, and they sat down and ordered coffee. Boone was casually glancing around the room. He saw a couple of the men whose names were on the list and pointed them out to Mitch. Another walked in while they were still sitting there. From Ellie's they headed for the Golden Monkey, and along the way Boone spotted another on the street. Inside the Monkey were two more.

They were just about to walk out again when a short man with a beard stopped Boone. "Hey," he said. "You get that new jailhouse all finished up?"

"Yeah, Andy," Boone said. "It's all done."

"Well, what'll you be working on next?"

"I'm going to do some work on the newspaper office starting tomorrow," Boone said. "Say, Andy, have you met the sheriff yet?"

The scrawny little man gave Mitch a curious look. "Can't say I have. Indian, ain't you?" he said.

"Apache," Mitch said. "That bother you?"

"Don't bother me none," Andy said. "You ever ride with Geronimo?"

"Quite a bit," said Mitch.

"What Mitch means," said Boone, "is that he rode after Geronimo. He was a scout under Crook. Don't you read the newspaper?"

"Nope," Lang said. "Got no use for them."

"Well, Mitch, this is Andy Lang," said Boone. "Andy, shake hands with Sheriff Mitch Frye."

"Howdy to you, Sheriff," Lang said. "Apache sheriff, huh? Guess you'll be locking me up in your new jail when I get too drunk on a Saturday night."

"I don't care how drunk you get," Mitch said, "as long as you don't get too rowdy."

"I'm a wild man when I get drunk," Lang said. "I roar and roar."

Lang headed for the bar. Mitch and Boone watched after him for a moment.

"He's all talk," Boone said. "He's harmless enough."

"Yeah?" Mitch said. "He's also wearing new boots."

Chapter Eighteen

Big Bob rode back into Paxton that night. He stopped at Ellie's for a bowl of beef stew and sat and ate alone. He was surly. He'd been feeling bad. He was lonesome. He missed George. He would never tell that to another soul, but it was the truth, and it hurt him deeply. Not only had he lost his partner and his only friend, but he had actually been accused of the murder. Slowly his sadness developed into anger. He thought that he had plenty of gold. He wasn't really sure what he would do with all of it. He thought that he would sell his claim, pack his plunder, and get the hell out of Paxton. Maybe go to California—or New York.

He finished his stew and paid for it, and when Ellie thanked him, he grunted at her. He walked straight to the Golden Monkey, up to the bar, and ordered himself a glass of whiskey. He pushed the tiny shot glass back at the bartender and demanded a serious drinking glass. The bartender put a tumbler on the bar in front of Bob, and, as Bob insisted, left the bottle. He hesitated, though, before walking away from his surly customer.

"Bob," he said, "I don't want no trouble from you like the last time."

"Get out of here and leave me alone," Bob growled. He picked up his tumbler and the bottle and walked to a table over by the wall. He sat with his back to the wall and scowled at everyone else in the room. He drank his whiskey in silence. He would clear out in the morning, he told himself, and it would be none too soon. He would clear out and never come back. He didn't want to see Paxton or anyone in it ever again. He would clear out immediately, except that he needed to settle his affairs, sell the claim, and he couldn't do that until in the morning. It was too late in the day. Besides that, he wanted to get drunk first. The morning would be soon enough. He drained the tumbler and refilled it.

Mitch sat behind his desk with all his notes, but he wasn't really looking at the notes. He was thinking about Andy Lang, a harmless-appearing little man. He was thinking about Lang's new boots, and the fact that Lang had been a frequent visitor and hanger-around while the new jail was being built. And it seemed to Mitch that when he had glanced at Lang's feet and noticed the new boots he had also gotten the distinct impression that for a little man, Lang had big feet.

He decided that he would look Lang up in the morning, first thing, and he would bring him to the office for questioning—and to try on the pair of boots. Lang had said that he didn't read the newspaper, but Mitch wondered now if that had been a lie. Likely he had read the paper and then thrown away the boots. Mitch wished that he had not mentioned the boots to Radin. But he was also thinking that, even if he could tie the boots to Lang, that would not be sufficient evidence to arrest the man. It would only prove that Lang had once visited George Orr or Big Bob, had spent time around the jail while it was under construction, which fact was already established by the evidence of four witnesses, and that he had come up to the jail the night the two prisoners escaped.

Mitch knew absolutely that the man in the boots had tossed the hacksaw, but he did not know if his testimony, and his reputation as an expert tracker, would hold up in a court of law. A defense attorney would answer that it was well known that Lang had been around the jail. His boot prints meant nothing more than that. If Lang was his man, Mitch knew, it would take more proof. And if Lang was the man and had read the paper, it would take more smoking out. The man was certainly giving every appearance of being his normal self. He did not seem panicked. He did not appear to be worried about anything.

Then the door flew open, and Reid came bursting into the office and into Mitch's thoughts. "You'd better get over to the Monkey," Reid said. "Big Bob's on another rampage."

Mitch jumped up from his chair and strapped on his Colt, then hurried out the door. Reid ran with him to the Golden Monkey. Apparently Bob had not started shooting yet. Mitch had heard no shots. But the Monkey had been emptied of customers—all except Big Bob. A quick look around showed Mitch that Bob had incapacitated one customer, for a man was sprawled on the floor, dead or unconscious. Of course, the man might be drunk and passed out, Mitch thought, not wanting to jump to conclusions.

A few tables were overturned and some chairs had been thrown around the room. Bob was standing at the bar, a bottle in his left hand and a chair in his right. He saw Mitch as Mitch stepped inside. "Get out of here," he shouted, and he flung the chair toward Mitch. It flew only about halfway across the room, crashing down on a table. Mitch walked on in, moving toward Bob.

"Bob," he said, "cut it out. Come along with me."

"So you can chain me up like a dog again?" Bob said. "Hell no."

"We've got a nice new jail all finished, Bob," Mitch said, moving in closer. "It'll be right comfortable for you in there. Come on, now. Don't give me no trouble."

"You stay away from me," Bob said. "This ain't none of your business. I ain't going to your new jail, neither."

"Bob," Mitch said, "you can't be tearing the place apart like this. Hurting folks. What happened to that man over there?"

"Him?" Bob said. "Aw, I just knocked him down. That's all. Now, get on out of here and leave me alone."

"I can't do that, Bob," Mitch said. "You've got to go on over to the jail with me."

"I warned you," said Bob, whipping the revolver out of its holster at his side. A shot roared, and the bullet tore at Mitch's left shoulder. Mitch acted on instinct. He pulled out his Colt, thumbing back the hammer as he drew it out, and squeezed the trigger as the revolver leveled. He didn't aim. He didn't have time. He pointed. There was another roar in the tent saloon, and Big Bob staggered from the impact of a slug hitting his chest. A look of surprise came over his face. He stood weaving for an instant, then fell back against the bar. His gun hand went limp, and he dropped his revolver.

"I was—I was going to leave town," he said, "in the morning."

Then he pitched forward on his face and lay there dead.

"Damn it," said Mitch. "Goddamn it."

Reid walked in and stepped over to Mitch's side. "You sure got him," he said.

"He didn't give me no choice," said Mitch.

"If he was the killer," said Reid, "then it's all over."

"It wasn't him," Mitch said.

"How do you know?" Reid demanded. "He was on your list."

"His feet's too big," said Mitch, and he turned to walk out of the saloon.

Mitch sat alone in Ellie's the next morning. He had finished his breakfast early. There had been only two customers in the place when he came in. He hadn't slept well the night before, so he was up and restless early. He was drinking coffee when Jewel came in. She walked right over to his table, a stern look on her face.

"Can I sit down," she said, "or do you want to be alone?"

"Go ahead," Mitch said. "I don't mind."

Jewel sat across from him. "Are you all right?" she said.

"He only nicked my shoulder," he said. "It's just a little sore. That's all."

"That's not what I meant," she said. "You killed a man last night."

"I've killed men before," Mitch said. "It ain't pleasant, but I can live with it."

Jewel studied Mitch's face for a moment, and in the silence Ellie walked up to the table.

"What'll you have, Jewel?" she said. "The usual? Eggs and ham?"

"Yes, thanks," Jewel said as Ellie put a cup of coffee in front of her. Ellie went off to fill the order. "You're a strange man, Mitch Frye," Jewel said.

"Yeah?" Mitch said.

"Yeah," she said. "You are. You're not mean, but you're hard and cold. Is it because you're Apache?"

"I don't know a damn thing about being Apache," Mitch told her. "All I know about Apaches I learned from white men—Al Sieber and Tom Horn and General Crook."

"But you are Apache, aren't you?" she asked.

"My old man was Apache," Mitch said. "I never knew him. My mother raised me among white people. I could always tell they didn't want me around, but that's how I was raised."

"I see," said Jewel.

"What do you see?"

"I can see how that would make you . . . the way you are."

"You mean hard and cold?" he said.

"Yes," she said. "That. And distant."

"A man tries to survive the best way he can," Mitch said.

"But isn't there more to life than just surviving?" Jewel asked.

"I don't know," said Mitch. "Is there?"

"I think so," she said. "There's making a good life for yourself. There's family and friends. There's—well, there's love, and marriage, and children. And there's doing good for others."

"Maybe for you," said Mitch, "but that's not for me."

"Why not?"

"Jewel," Mitch said, "the Apaches don't want me. Hell, if they could get their hands on me, they'd kill me. And whites don't want me around. If I wasn't the sheriff, and if your old man didn't want me for sheriff, I'd be run out of this town in a minute. White folks don't want Apaches around. The nearest thing I ever had to home was the Army, and now they don't want me either."

Ellie came back with Jewel's breakfast and a coffeepot. She put down the plate and then refilled the two cups on the table. "Thanks," Jewel said.

"You need anything else?" Ellie asked.

"No, thanks," Jewel said. Ellie left again, and Jewel looked deep into Mitch's face. Mitch looked down at his cup. "Times change," she said. "People change. You're at home here, aren't you? You have a place to live. You have a job. You have friends, at least a few. You hardly ever eat alone. You've got the respect of the community."

"It ain't home," said Mitch.

"Come on, Mitch," she said. "Aren't you beginning to feel at least a little more comfortable here in Paxton?"

"Jewel," he said, "if your old man would turn me loose, I'd leave here right this minute."

She started to eat her breakfast, wishing that she could think of something more to say to him, wishing that she could convince him that he could have a good life in Paxton, that he already had a good life, if he could only accept it and learn to enjoy it. But she could think of no more words to use on him, and just then her father walked in. He gave them a stern look and walked over to sit at the table with them.

Chapter Nineteen

"You two seem to be seeing an awful lot of each other lately," Reid said.

"We're just visiting, Daddy," Jewel said.

"I told you both I don't like this," said Reid.

Ellie came hurrying up to the table. "Breakfast, Mr. Reid?" she asked.

"Not now," he said, dismissing her curtly. She went away. "I don't ask a hell of a lot of you, Jewel. You're headstrong, and you've always had your own way, but—"

"So don't try changing things now," she said. Her face flushed a little. "You're not going to start telling me who I can and cannot talk to. Are you?"

"I don't mean it that way," Reid said, suddenly on the defensive. "I just—"

"Well, how do you mean it, then?" she said.

"I know how he means it," said Mitch. "He's afraid if you talk to me, it might lead to something else, and he don't want no half-breed Apache messing around with his daughter. That's it, ain't it, Reid?''

"I, uh, I just don't think that it's a good idea to—"

"Forget it, Daddy," Jewel said. "We're just—We just talk. I started to say we're just friends, but I'm not sure about even that. I don't think he really even likes me."

"I never said that," Mitch protested.

"You don't have to say it," she said.

"It's your old man I don't like," Mitch said. Now Reid flushed with anger. "I told you before, Reid," Mitch went on, "you can always fire me. I'll leave town the same minute, and you'll never see me again."

"Go to hell," said Reid.

"Daddy!" Jewel said.

"Likely I will," said Mitch, "sooner or later. You going to have some breakfast or not?"

"Hell," said Reid, "I might as well."

Mitch raised a hand to get Ellie's attention.

They had finished their meals and were on their way out, Reid well ahead of the other two, when a scruffy, bearded man in dirty clothes with the look of a miner stopped Reid. The two men had a hasty conversation. Reid shushed the man, looked over his shoulder, and waved Mitch forward. Mitch caught up, and Reid said, "Brisket, this is Sheriff Mitch Frye. Mitch, this is Brisket. You need to hear him out—over at your office. Let's go."

"I know who the killer is," Brisket said. "And I know that I'm next on his list. He's going to kill me, and then he'll be done. He'll be done, and he'll get out of here, and you'll never catch him."

"Slow down," Mitch said, drawing on his cigarette. "First off, who is it?"

"His name's Sandy Connors," said Brisket, "but I don't know what name he's going by here."

"Have you seen him in town?" said Mitch.

131

"No," said Brisket, "but I know it's him. I'm next on the list."

"Describe him for us," Mitch said.

"Well, he's, uh, he's about your size, I'd say. Yeah. Kind of husky too, you know," Brisket said. "He's got sandy hair. That's why we called him Sandy. Blue eyes. Kind of watery. I don't know what else to say. Oh. He's about my age, I guess. Forty maybe."

Mitch was surprised at the age reference. He would have taken Brisket to be much older. The shaggy hair and beard did that, he guessed. He tried to picture the old fart with a shave and a haircut. "Do you know anything more about him?" Mitch asked. "Does he have a profession?"

"He was some kind of clerk, I think, before . . ."

"Before what?" Mitch said.

"Well, before I met up with him, I guess is what I meant to say."

"Where did you know him?" Mitch said.

"Back east."

"What makes you think he's here in Paxton?" said Reid, suddenly injecting himself into the discussion.

"There's no one else would be killing us," said Brisket. "Them others and me."

"What's the connection between you and the murder victims?" Mitch asked.

"Well, uh, we all knowed each other back east," said Brisket. "That's all I can tell you. But it's Sandy. He's killed them all but me, and I'm next. Believe me. I know what I'm talking about. I know it's him. He's here somewhere. He's just waiting to get his chance to kill me and finish off the job. You got to protect me, Sheriff."

"Where do you live?" Mitch asked.

"I got a place down the road a ways," said Brisket.

"A claim?"

"Yeah. That's right. A claim."

Mitch shot a hard look toward Reid. "It ain't on my map," he said. Reid shrugged. "Brisket," Mitch said, "just what do you want me to do? I don't know this Sandy Connors, and you haven't even seen him in town. You won't tell me why Connors is killing miners or what connection you have with the others. You want me to move in with you, or what?''

"You're the law," said Brisket. "It's your job to find him and arrest him. It's your job to protect me. Hell, I told you who it is. That's half the job done for you. What kind of a sheriff are you, anyway?" He faced Reid. "What kind of a sheriff did you hire here, Reid? A damned Indian. What kind of law is that? I want protection."

"Brisket," said Reid, "Mitch is right. You're holding back information that we need here to solve this case. Mitch can't protect you if you don't tell him everything you know."

"Ain't there some kind of law in this country that says I don't have to say nothing that will get me into trouble with the law?" said Brisket. "Ain't there some kind of law like that?"

Mitch looked questioningly at Reid.

"He's talking about the Fifth Amendment to the Constitution of the United States," Reid said. "And he's right."

"See there," said Brisket. "I don't have to tell you no more than what I already told you."

"On the grounds that it might tend to incriminate you," said Reid.

"What?" said Brisket.

"If you tell more, you might get yourself in trouble with the law," Reid explained.

"Oh," said Brisket. "Yeah. That's it."

Mitch walked over to the window and tossed out the butt of his cigarette. "We're talking in circles," he said. "All right. You don't have to tell me no more, but if you don't tell me no more, then there's nothing I can do for you. I could put you in jail, though."

"Put me in jail?" Brisket roared indignantly. "For what?"

"For your protection," said Mitch.

"It's called protective custody," Reid said. "There's also

such a thing as holding in custody a material witness.''

"I ain't going to jail," Brisket said.

"All right, Brisket," said Mitch. "Let's you and me take a walk around town. See if you spot this Sandy Connors anywhere. If you spot him, I can arrest him. Then there won't be no need to hold you in jail for your protection. Come on.''

"Go on," said Reid. "I'll be in my office."

Mitch and Brisket made the rounds, but Brisket never spotted Sandy Connors. No one but Mitch, Reid, and Brisket knew that Connors was being looked for, and Mitch said nothing to anyone. There would be no use in mentioning the name, he figured, because even if Connors really was in Paxton, he would be using some other name like everyone else. At last Mitch gave up the search.

"Let's go back," he said.

"To jail?" said Brisket.

"You can go home or go to jail," said Mitch. "I don't give a damn, but if you go home, there's not much I can do for you.''

"Will I be locked in?" Brisket asked.

"I won't lock the door if you don't want me to," said Mitch, "but locks keep people out, too."

"Tell you what, Sheriff," Brisket said. "I'll come around just before dark. You can lock me in for the night. How's that?"

Mitch shrugged. "Suits me," he said.

Mitch was walking back to his office when Jewel spotted him from inside the general store. She ran out to meet him. "What was all that about?" she asked.

"You mean that old dodger called Brisket?" Mitch said.

"Yeah," she said. "What else?"

As they walked along, Mitch gave Jewel the rundown on Brisket's tale. When he had finished, they were inside the office again. Mitch sat behind his desk and Jewel perched herself on top of it. "All right," she said, "so there is a connection."

Mitch took out a clean sheet of paper and started a new list.

Sandy Connors
Howard Jones
George Orr
Red Calhoun
Billy Whitehead
Brisket

"If Brisket's telling it straight," he said, "these men all have something in common from the past, from somewhere back east. For some reason or other, Connors has got it in for the rest of them, and he's set about killing them off. We may have Connors's right name, but all we got on the rest are aliases."

"The newspaper story did smoke someone out," Jewel said. "And you know more now than you did before."

"But not enough to act on," Mitch said. "I still don't know what I can do, unless Brisket spots Connors or I actually catch Connors in the act of trying to kill Brisket. I don't know the man if I was to see him, and I don't know what name he's going by."

"Um," Jewel mused. "It's a tough one, all right. Will you keep Brisket in protective custody?"

"That's the second time I've heard that expression today," Mitch said. "You and your old man both lawyers, or what?"

"Oh, never mind that," she said. "Will you?"

"I offered," said Mitch. "He wants to run loose during daylight and come in to get locked up after dark."

"You think that will be good enough?" she asked.

"Long as he's smart enough to stay in town, it ought to be," Mitch said. "Connors, if he's the man, has killed all the others out at their claims. Brisket ought to be safe in town and in daylight."

"Yeah. I guess so," Jewel said. "But what will Connors do if he doesn't get a chance at Brisket out at the claim?"

"If he wants him bad enough," said Mitch, "he might just have to show himself. Try something in town in the daylight, or try to get to him in jail at night."

"That's smoking him out," she said. "Right?"

"Right," said Mitch. "If it works. If it don't, we just get another man killed. Say, would you like a cup of coffee?"

"It's a little soon after breakfast for me," she said, "but . . . sure. Why not?"

They walked back over to Ellie's, found a table, sat and ordered coffee. Ellie wasn't very busy. Most of the breakfast crowd had gone. She brought their coffee right away, and they drank a first cup each in silence. Ellie refilled their cups for them and went about her business of cleaning tables, getting ready for the next rush, which would come at lunchtime.

"Mitch," said Jewel, breaking the long silence, "why'd you bring me back over here?"

"The sheriff's office ain't a comfortable place to sit and visit," he said.

"You haven't said a word since we've been here," she said.

"I did just now."

"But why did you bring me over here?" she asked again.

"This is the best place I know of in town to just sit and drink coffee," he said.

"Why did you bring me along? Just for company? That's not like you," she said.

"Well," Mitch said, "it was something you said this morning to your old man."

Jewel leaned toward Mitch across the table, and her eyes probed his face. "What?" she said.

"Ah, hell," he said, "I really do like you, Jewel."

Chapter Twenty

Brisket staggered into Mitch's office at sundown. He was carrying a bottle by the neck, and it was almost full, so he had already gotten himself drunk, then bought a fresh bottle to take with him for the night. "Lock me up, Sheriff Apache," he said. "Lock me up safe and snug for the night."

Mitch stood up, taking some keys off his desktop. "Come on," he said.

Brisket held his bottle high for Mitch to see. "Any objections?" he said.

"I can't see no harm in it," said Mitch. "If you make a mess in my cell, you clean it up."

Mitch led the way out back, Brisket following. He unlocked the door to the new jailhouse and went inside. "When I leave," he said, "I'll lock that door again." He opened a cell door to admit Brisket. Brisket hesitated a moment, then went into the cell. He stood in the middle of the room and looked around.

"All the comforts of home," he said. "This will do nicely."

Mitch showed Brisket that the barred windows were also equipped with inside shutters made of heavy wood that could be latched from inside. "You keep these shut and latched," he said. "I'll lock the cell door and the outside door. You'll be safe enough. I'll look in on you before I go to breakfast."

"If I'm sleeping soundly," said Brisket, "don't bother me."

Mitch went out, locking the cell door, then he left the jailhouse and locked the outside door. He went back into his office. Brisket aggravated him. The old son of a bitch knew a hell of a lot more than he was telling. What could those six men have done together or had in common, and what could five of them have done to make the sixth angry enough at them to kill them off one by one? What were all of them doing in Paxton? Brisket could answer all of those questions if he only would, but apparently his answers would incriminate him, make him liable for arrest and punishment—for what? Something all six men had done together somewhere back east? So it would seem. And who was Sandy Connors, and where was he?

And damn it, it seemed it was not legal for him to try to compel the bastard to talk. Mitch hadn't known that. Even old Brisket had known it. He hadn't put it in the same fancy lawyer words as had Reid and Jewel, but he sure as hell knew the concept. Mitch was thinking that he had no business in this sheriff's job, but then, how was he going to convince Reid of that very obvious fact?

Reid had laid his trap for Mitch meticulously, and he was determined to keep Mitch in it now that he had him there. Why, Mitch wondered. He was a good manhunter. He knew that. But the sheriff's job called for a man*handler,* someone who could stop fights and shove drunks into jail. This string of killings was not the usual business of a town sheriff. And even if it was, the way of dealing with it was not anywhere in Mitch's experience. What the hell did Reid want him for, anyway?

138

He tired of sitting at his desk, and decided that it was late enough to call it a night. Instead of going to bed, though, he dragged a chair into the hallway, propped it against the wall by the back door, which he opened, and sat in it. He dozed off and on there by the back door. If anyone came up to the jail and tried to get in, he would hear the noise.

It was about two o'clock in the morning when the explosion woke him up. He straightened up with a start. The first thing he did was check the jail. The door was locked. All was quiet there. He ran around the building and looked down the street. He could see flames at the lower end of town, and in the weird light cast by the flames, he could see figures running in the street. He ran toward them.

In the crowd he saw J. Paxton Reid. "What the hell was that?" he said.

"Dynamite," said Reid. "Someone blew up the mining supplies store down here."

"Anyone see who did it?" Mitch asked.

"Not that I know of," said Reid. "Right now we have to organize a bucket brigade to keep that fire from spreading."

Together Mitch and Reid got the crowd organized and got the water buckets going down the line. They worked until daylight before the flames were entirely quenched and they felt safe leaving it alone. Reid sat down heavily on the board sidewalk, and Mitch dropped down beside him. Jewel saw them there and walked over to join them.

"What the hell would anyone want to blow that place up for?" Mitch asked.

"Who knows?" Reid said. "Maybe he had a big bill and didn't want to pay it. Maybe he had a grudge against Falwell, the owner. I don't know."

"Could it have been an accident?" Jewel asked.

"I doubt it," said Reid. "Well, I'm going home to clean up."

He stood up and walked away without another word. Mitch figured that he'd do the same thing, except he had no place at home to clean up in. He would have to get some clean clothes and carry them to the bathhouse, and it was

139

liable to be busy, since so many men had gotten involved in fighting the fire. It was hot and dirty work.

He walked back to his office and living quarters, picked up clean clothes, and then walked to the bathhouse. He had been right. There was a line. He waited his turn patiently. It was an hour before he got back to the office and walked out to the jail to check on Brisket. He unlocked the door and walked inside. Moving over to the cell where he had left Brisket, the first thing he noticed were the open shutters. The damned fool, he thought. Then he saw the body lying on the floor, the head in a pool of blood.

"The way I figure it," Mitch was saying, "Sandy Connors blew that dynamite to get me away from the jail. We'll likely never know how he got Brisket to open up them shutters. Maybe the damn fool just opened them up for fresh air. I don't know. Anyhow, Connors got the whole town down at the other end, then he came up to the jail and shot Brisket through the window."

"It could have happened like that," Reid agreed. They were sitting in Ellie's—Mitch, Reid, Jewel, and Jasper Boone. They had all finished their breakfasts and were sipping more coffee.

"How else would he have got me away from the jail so he could get at Brisket?" Mitch said. "And why else would anyone have blown up that store? It got me clean to the other end of town. It's too much coincidence. It was planned. I'm sure of it."

"And now there's no one in town who knows this Connors," Boone said.

"Just Connors himself, is all," said Mitch.

"What can you do?" Jewel asked.

"I don't know," Mitch said. "According to what Brisket told me, Connors's job is done. Likely he'll leave town or just settle down to an ordinary life. He won't be doing nothing more suspicious. I don't see how we can find him out now."

"We'll just have a killer walking around among us as free as the breeze," said Jewel.

"If your theory is right about that bunch all having been involved in something together back east," Boone said, "maybe they deserved what they got."

"It don't look good on my office, though," said Mitch. "Besides, if they was all involved in it together, then Connors was as bad as the rest. I don't like it."

"Involved in what?" Boone said.

"Hell," said Mitch. "I don't know."

"One thing we can do," Reid said, "we can watch for anyone leaving town real sudden."

"Yeah," said Mitch. "We can do that."

When they decided to break it up, Mitch asked a last question of Reid. "Is there a place in town," he said, "that has a record of all the mining claims, where they're at and who owns them?"

"Yes. Of course," Reid said. "What are you up to?"

"I just want to study on them some," Mitch said. "I ain't sure why."

He was exactly sure of what he wanted to know and what he wanted to do, but he didn't want to tell anyone about it. He was tired of letting his plans be known and then having them lead nowhere. This time, he decided, he'd keep it to himself. Then, if it led somewhere, he would tell the others. Reid showed him the records office, and Mitch looked up the location of Brisket's claim. He got the directions firmly in his mind, returned the book to the clerk, and left the office.

He had searched the shacks of all the victims except Brisket, not counting Jones, of course. Jones had worked for the Paxton. He had looked into what personal belongings Jones had left behind. So far he had found nothing. Even so, he wanted to search the shack on the claim of old Brisket. He might find something there. He didn't want to sneak out of town. On the other hand, he didn't want to call attention to himself, didn't want to answer questions about where he was going. He decided that he would just have to ride out and take his chances.

141

He walked to his office and went inside. Then he walked through the building and out the back door. He walked behind all the buildings all the way to Sam Neely's stable and went in Neely's back door. "Hey, Sam," he called out.

Neely came peering down the passageway to see who had called.

"Damn, Sheriff," he said. "What for you sneaking in back doors?"

"I ain't sneaking, Sam," Mitch said. "I just happened to walk in that way. That bother you?"

"Don't bother me none," Neely said. "What do you want?"

"Want my horse saddled up," said Mitch.

Neely set to work. "What about that goddamned explosion last night?" he said. "It like to scared the hell out of me. Woke me out of a sweet dream, too. I was riding a real pretty little whore, and then the whole world blew up. Goddamn it. You know who done it?"

"I have an idea," Mitch said.

"You going to get the son of a bitch?"

"I'm going to try."

"Well," said Neely, "I hope you do catch him. Son of a bitch spoiled my dream."

Neely tightened the cinch and his job was done. He handed the reins to Mitch.

"Thanks, Sam," Mitch said, and he led the horse out the back door. Outside, he mounted and rode behind the buildings to the other end of town. Once past the last tents and shanties, he took to the main road. He knew that he had a long ride ahead of him that day. The trail to Brisket's shack took off from the road about halfway down the mountain. The trip and the search would take most of the rest of the day. He would have to spend the night in Brisket's shack or somewhere along the road.

But this was a last chance. He was hoping to find something among the possessions of Brisket that would be a clue to the identities of the dead men he knew only by their aliases and to the common thread that ran through their lives, something that would lead him to Sandy Connors and perhaps a motive for the killings. It was a long shot. There had been nothing at the other murder sites. But then, he thought, Brisket's shack was not the site of a murder, for Brisket had been killed in jail. He had a sudden thought. Perhaps there had been something at the murder sites, and the murderer had taken it, being careful to leave the places looking as if they had not been ransacked. Maybe he would find something at Brisket's place after all. Maybe. He surely needed something at this point. Time was now on the side of Connors.

Chapter Twenty-one

The shack seemed to be clinging to the side of the mountain precariously. Mitch wondered what it must have been like for the original builder and why he had chosen such a location. He looked around and found the answer for himself. There was not a flat spot in sight. He supposed that the place must have been built because the original miner was digging nearby, but he didn't see the mine. This place was even more remote and more isolated than was that of Billie Whitehead. The trail to the place was more difficult, steeper and more narrow, a rocky trail that seemed almost unused.

Mitch urged his horse on up close to the shack and dismounted. The shack hung over him ominously. There below the shack was a small enclosure, scarcely a corral, more like a pen. The rails had fallen and the posts were leaning. Mitch lapped the reins around one of the sagging rails and looked up toward the shack. A narrow and steep stairway rose up just to his left. He mounted the stairs. They creaked with each careful step he took.

144

At last he reached the narrow landing at the top, and he pushed the door. It opened slowly. Mitch stood for a moment looking into the darkness of the wretched shack. Then he stepped inside. The atmosphere was heavy and musty. He seemed to be breathing dust. He stood still looking around, waiting for his eyes to adjust to the dim light. He spotted a lantern on a table and moved easily over to it. There were matches there beside it. He struck one and lit the lamp, then adjusted the flame.

The room was cluttered. Clothes were scattered. A couple of newspapers were on the table along with some dirty dishes. Shelves on the wall held tins of food. There was a coffeepot on top of a woodstove, and Mitch couldn't help wondering what trouble it had been getting that stove up those narrow steps. A narrow bed sat against one wall, its covers rumpled. There was only one chair in the room. Brisket and whoever had lived there before him had not anticipated guests.

Mining tools leaned against the wall in the corners of the room. An old pair of boots sat beside the bed. Several empty whiskey bottles had been discarded at various places around the room. Mitch found no real sign of successful mining, no stash of nuggets or dust. The shovel and the pick showed no signs of recent use. It seemed as if Brisket, like Red Calhoun, had used the claim only as a place to live. So where was he getting his money? The shack had a good supply of food, and Brisket seemed to get all the whiskey he wanted.

Mitch glanced at the papers on the table. One of them was the first issue of Radin's *Gazette*. That made sense. Brisket had read the story Mitch had given Radin and had figured out from the details in it that Connors was killing all that group of which he, too, was a part. The newspaper story had brought Brisket to town to see Reid and demand protection. Mitch looked at the other paper casually and noticed that it was from St. Louis, Missouri.

Connors and the rest had known each other "back east," and from the way Brisket had talked, Mitch believed that the reason for the killings was something that had happened back there. Perhaps in Missouri. Mitch shoved the chair up to the table and sat down. He moved the lantern slightly for better light, and he unfolded the Missouri paper. Right there on the front page was a photograph of Red Calhoun.

There was no doubt about it. It was Red Calhoun, all right, but the caption underneath the photo identified the man as Elmer Cook. Mitch felt a sudden thrill. Now he was getting somewhere. The accompanying story bore the headline COOK GANG ELUDES POSSE. Mitch read the following story:

> The notorious gang of outlaws led by the outlaw Elmer Cook fled westerly with the loot from their latest caper with a posse headed by Sheriff Johnson McMasters hot on their heels. Unfortunately, McMasters lost their trail. For now, the gang has escaped the clutches of the law.
>
> As most of our readers are undoubtedly aware, the Cook gang robbed the First State Bank at Central City of well over $100,000. Known members of the gang are Elmer Cook, himself, Vance Gordon, Skip Horner, Sam Barrett, Goose Roberts, and Sandy Connors.

There it was, the whole sordid tale. There were only two things missing now. First, what had happened to turn Connors against the others? Second, and most important, who, in Paxton, was Sandy Connors? Mitch sat in deep thought. There had to be some way to smoke Connors out. He sure couldn't think of one, though. All the men on Connors's list, all the former gang members, were now dead. Mitch wondered about the money. Had they split it up before coming to Paxton? If so, that explained how Red Calhoun and Brisket had been living so well without working. It explained the mining claims used as nothing but fronts.

He thought that he could send a wire to Sheriff McMasters informing him that Sandy Connors was known to be in the vicinity of Paxton, that the rest of the gang was known to be dead, and that, unfortunately, the whereabouts of the missing money was still unknown. He would do that, he decided, but it wouldn't really solve the problem. It would take time to get any helpful reaction from McMasters, and by that time Connors could be well away from Paxton. As far as Mitch could tell, there was nothing now to keep him around. Ah, well, at least he knew his next step. That was more than he had known for some time.

He folded the Missouri newspaper up and tucked it inside his shirt. Then he left the shack. It was already dusk outside. Mitch knew that he didn't want to spend a night in the precariously perched shack, though, and there wasn't really any place fit to settle down for the night in the near vicinity. He decided to try to make it back to the main road. If he had to, he could sleep beside the road down there.

He was about halfway back to the road, and it was already full dark and cold. He thought about unrolling his blanket and throwing it over his shoulders, but he kept riding. He could stand it until he made it the rest of the way down to the road. Then a shot echoed through the night air, and Mitch felt the bite of a hot bullet high on his left shoulder. His startled horse reared, and Mitch lost the saddle, tumbling to the narrow trail and sliding off the side. The frightened horse ran on toward the road without its rider.

Mitch was on foot, without his rifle and without his blanket. He was not even wearing a jacket. He was a long walk from Paxton, even from the nearest occupied mine shack, and he was wounded. He thought that the wound was slight, but it was bleeding. It would have its effect on his stamina. He found himself a fairly secure perch there on the sloping side of the trail and unholstered his Colt. He searched ahead for any sign of the shooter. He could see nothing out there in the dark. It must be Connors, though, he told himself. Who else would it be?

He tried to figure what to do, but he could think of nothing. It would be suicide to move out onto the road. The bushwhacker knew just about where Mitch was, and Mitch had no idea where to look for his attacker. Sitting there was foolish also. If Connors saw him drop, he would have a pretty good idea where to look to finish the job. Mitch looked over his shoulder, down the side of the drop-off. He could tell nothing about it in the darkness. Still, it was the only way to go.

Slowly, carefully, he moved a foot downward, feeling for a firm place to plant it. He inched his way down into the black unknown. He holstered the Colt so he would have both hands free, and it was a good thing, too, for he slipped once, and had to clutch desperately with both hands to keep from sliding free into the black hole beneath him. He kept inching his way down, wondering how far he would have to go before he found something solid and more or less level on which to stand.

The rip on his shoulder was burning, and he could feel the blood still running freely. He hoped that he would not grow too weak from loss of blood to continue his descent. He needed his strength, but he could not afford to hurry. He had to be patient. He had to feel his way every inch. He kept moving, straining every muscle in his body. He was well beyond the reach of Connors now. No one would try to follow him down that slope. Now he was concentrating on his descent, on finding toeholds and solid rocks and bits of brush in the darkness, finding them by feel. All of sudden, there was nothing. The slope turned abruptly into a straight wall, smooth and slick, and he fell, and for an instant he thought that he had come to the end of his life, but only for an instant. He hit the ground hard. It stunned him, but that was all. He was at the bottom.

Mitch woke up with the sunrise. He woke up shivering from the night cold. He sat up and looked around, but he saw nothing familiar. He stood and walked away from the slope he had come down the night before. Turning, he looked up toward the trail he had left, and he could see more or less the way it ran. Then, looking ahead of where he stood, he figured the direction he must walk to find his way back to the main road. He checked to make sure his Colt was still at his side. It was. He started walking.

His legs felt weak from the strain of the descent. He was sore all over, and he could tell that the loss of blood had sapped some of his strength. He knew that he had a long walk ahead of him, though, so he kept moving. After a while, he could tell that the walking was loosening his tight muscles. He was feeling a little better. He was still cold, and he was hungry, but he had suffered that and more before, and he had survived. He kept walking.

By the time the sun was high enough to begin warming the day, Mitch came across a pool of fresh water. The water was running down from above, and out of the pool it turned into a small stream. It was clear and it was cold, and Mitch drank all he could hold. It didn't kill the hunger pangs, but it helped. He stepped across the stream and started walking again toward the road. That son of a bitch Connors, he thought. He wished that he knew who Connors was. He longed to kill the man.

He walked on, and he thought that if he ever found Connors, and if Connors refused to fight, he would be obligated, as sheriff, to arrest the man and hold him for trial. He hoped that Connors would resist arrest, that he would want to fight. He wanted the chance to kill the man himself. He felt he deserved that opportunity.

Chapter Twenty-two

Mitch rode into Paxton in the back end of the regular supply wagon. He had been picked up on the road earlier in the day, after the driver had seen him lying beside the road hurt and apparently exhausted. The wagon pulled up in front of Reid's office, and the driver went inside to get the mayor. Reid had Mitch carried to his own bed in the back room of the sheriff's office, and then he sent for a doctor. When Mitch woke up in his own bed, he soon realized that he had been stripped and bathed and his wound had been dressed. He saw Jewel in the room sitting in a chair watching him, and he was embarrassed knowing that he was naked under the sheet, and the two of them were alone together in the room. He wondered just who had undressed and bathed him.

"Well, hello," she said, noticing that he had at last opened his eyes. "You slept for a long time. I was beginning to worry about you."

"Is it dark outside again?" he asked.

"Yes," she said, "for the second time since we put you to bed."

"You mean I've slept a day and a night?" he asked.

"Something like that," she said. "When they brought you in it was late in the day. You were asleep in the wagon. You slept all that night and all of today. How do you feel?"

"Weak," he said, "and hungry."

"I'll run over to Ellie's and get you something," she said. "You stay right where you are."

Mitch thought that she hadn't needed to tell him to stay put. He didn't feel like getting up. Not just yet. He'd had plenty of sleep, but he was still groggy from so much of it, and he didn't have the strength to get up and do anything anyway. Besides, he was so hungry that the promise of food being brought to him was enough to keep him still. Jewel was back soon, saying that Ellie would bring over some stew and coffee. She also told him that Reid was on his way. "We were both worried about you," she said.

"You and your old man?" said Mitch with a wry smile.

"Yes," she said, "both of us. And others, too. Ellie. Jasper Boone and Mr. Radin."

"Oh. Well, thanks," he said. "I'll be all right."

He didn't really believe that anyone was too worried about him. Not many people in Mitch's life had ever really worried about him. His mother, when he was young and still with her, Sieber and Horn. No one else. He could believe that Jewel had worried, though. He could believe that. But Reid? He'd been worried that he might lose his captive sheriff. That's all. Boone and Ellie? He didn't think so. Not really. Ellie finally came in with a bowl of stew, a pot of coffee and a cup, and a hunk of bread on a tray, and Jewel helped Mitch sit up so he could eat. Ellie placed the tray on his lap. "Anything else I can do for you?" she asked.

"No, thank you, Ellie," Mitch said. "This looks great."

As he started eating stew and bread, Jewel poured the cup full of coffee. Just then Reid walked into the room. "Ah, awake and eating, I see," he said. "Good." Mitch kept eating. "We found the newspaper you were carrying," Reid continued. "Good work. It explains a lot about this case. Where'd you find it? Brisket's shack would be my guess, judging from where you were found."

Mitch muttered an affirmative and kept eating.

"Daddy," said Jewel, "let him eat. The questions can wait a few minutes."

"Oh, hell," said Reid. "All right. Then you don't need to talk, Mitch. Just listen. The way I figure it, Brisket told the truth. He just didn't tell it all. This Sandy Connors is the killer, all right. The murder victims are all men we knew under aliases. They were actually all members of the Cook gang. For some reason or other, this Connors had it in for the rest of the gang, and now he's killed them all. The man we knew as Red Calhoun was really Elmer Cook. We don't know which of the other names belongs to which of our victims, but we can be sure that they were the other gang members.

"Now, I guess that after you made this discovery out at Brisket's shack, Connors waylaid you. He shot you and scared your horse off. Oh, by the way, your horse was found. He's back at the stable." Reid paused and looked at his daughter. "I didn't ask a single question," he said.

Mitch finished the stew and bread and took a long swig of coffee.

"Who took off my clothes and washed me?" he asked.

"The doc did," Reid said.

"Well," said Mitch, "you got it all figured right. At least, you got it figured the same way I do. Only thing is, we don't know who Connors is, and he ain't likely to do nothing more to give himself away now that he's killed his men."

"At least we can assume that no one else in or around Paxton is in any danger from him," Reid said.

"The other thing we don't know is what become of the money they stole," Mitch said.

"Oh yeah," said Reid.

"Has anyone you know of left town?" Mitch asked.

"Not that I know of," said Reid.

"I think you ought to send a wire to that sheriff in Missouri," Mitch said. "Tell him what happened and what we found out here. Tell him that as far as we know, Connors is still around, but we can't identify him."

"Yes," Reid said. "We should do that. I'll take care of it."

"I have an idea," Jewel said. "We could still smoke him out."

"How?" Reid demanded.

"With another newspaper story," she said. "Let Connors know how much we know. Let him know that we know his name and that we know he's the killer. And let him know that the authorities back in Missouri have been notified. We might even say in the story, whether it's true or not, that someone from Missouri is coming out here to identify him."

"It might work," Mitch said.

"Hell," said Reid, "it will work."

"Let's hold off on that story a bit," Mitch said. "Let's at least wait till we get an answer to our wire."

"How come?" Reid asked.

"Smoking him out's one thing," said Mitch. "Spooking him's another. We can't stop every man who decides to leave town. And we can't hold anyone just for that reason either. What would we do? Lock up every man who tries to leave town and then try to figure out which one is Connors?"

"I see what you mean," Jewel said. "Maybe it wasn't such a great idea."

"It's a good idea," Mitch said. "Just not yet."

Reid had taken a notepad and pencil out of his pocket and was writing. In a moment he quit, and said, "How's this? We have reason to believe Sandy Connors is in Paxton. All other members of Cook gang are dead. Unfortunately, we cannot identify Connors. Can you advise?"

"That ought to do it," Mitch said.

"I'll go send it right now," said Reid, and he hurried out the door. Mitch looked at Jewel.

"I'm hungry," he said.

153

*   *   *

He ate another bowl of stew and another hunk of bread, and he drank the whole pot of coffee. Then he asked Jewel to find his makings, and he rolled himself a cigarette and smoked it. Reid came back with an answer to the wire he had sent. He read it to the other two. "U.S. Marshal Parker Robinson is en route to Paxton. He can identify Connors."

"That information would spook Connors for sure," said Mitch. "If he got ahold of that, he'd leave town right quick. We can't put that in the paper."

"Let's give Radin the whole story," Reid said, "except we'll leave out the part about the two wires."

"I don't see no harm in that," Mitch said.

The next morning Mitch got himself up and out of bed, dressed himself, and walked over to Ellie's. Inside the tent, Jewel jumped up when she saw him walk in. Leaving her unfinished meal on the table, she rushed to meet him. "You shouldn't be up," she said.

"I'm all right," Mitch said.

"I was planning to go over to see you in a little while," she said. "I didn't want to go too early, in case you were still sleeping."

"I'm all right," he said. "That bullet only nicked me. All I needed was some sleep, and I guess I got plenty of that. Let's go sit down. I'm hungry."

They moved to the table Jewel had abandoned and sat down. Ellie came and got Mitch's order. After remarking on his quick recovery, she went to fill it. Just then Jasper Boone walked in. "You two mind if I join you?" he asked.

"Sit down, Jasper," Mitch said.

"I heard you ran into some kind of trouble," Jasper said, taking a seat. "I'm glad to see you looking all right."

"It wasn't much trouble," Mitch said. "Some dry gulcher took a shot at me. Nicked my shoulder."

"Did you see who it was?" asked Boone.

"No," Mitch said. "It was dark, and I never laid eyes on him. The worst of it was that my horse bolted and I had to

154

walk back. I did get picked up on the main road.''

"Any suspects?" Boone asked.

Mitch shrugged. "Maybe the killer I been hunting," he said. "Maybe someone else. I don't know."

Jewel gave Mitch a curious look, but she kept her mouth shut. Ellie brought Mitch his breakfast and took an order from Boone. "This place sure keeps her jumping," Boone said.

"She does a good job," Mitch said.

Reid walked in, and he was talking before he sat down. "The story will be in the paper tomorrow morning," he said.

"What story?" Boone asked.

"Just about your sheriff getting shot off his horse like a greenhorn," Mitch said. "That's all." Reid took the hint and said no more. "Hell," Mitch went on, "if I was you, I'd fire the sheriff and get me one who can keep his horse. That story will be all over town by this time tomorrow. Be downright embarrassing, I'd say."

"I think the town will be willing to give the sheriff another chance," Reid said. "No harm's done. We got the sheriff and the horse back."

"Say," Mitch said. "Did anyone clean up the jail cell?"

"I had it done," Reid said.

Not much more was said while they finished their meals. Boone excused himself and left. Jewel looked at her father but spoke to Mitch. "I'm planning to cook a meal this evening," she said, "and I'm a good cook when I put my mind to it. I want you to join us for supper."

Reid scowled, but Jewel held his stare. Mitch saw their looks. He smiled. "What time?" he asked.

"Make it around six," Jewel said, and she got up to leave. Reid stared hard at Mitch for another moment, then got up and left without another word. Mitch called for more coffee.

Chapter Twenty-three

Mitch told himself that Jewel Reid sure didn't lie about her abilities. She was a real fine cook, yes, indeed. He swore that he hadn't had such a good meal in—well, he couldn't recall ever having had such a good meal. There wasn't much conversation at the dinner table while they were eating. Reid was sulky, and when he had cleaned up his own plate, he left the room in a silent huff with a scowl on his face. Mitch helped Jewel clear the table and offered to help her wash the dishes, but she wouldn't hear of it. She told him that the dishes could wait. Then she took him by the hand and led him out the front door to a porch swing, where they sat down together. There was a slight breeze in the cool night air.

Mitch had a sudden rush of mixed feelings. He was beginning to get the not-so-subtle hint that this beautiful young woman was interested in being, well, more than just his friend. And under any other circumstances, he would have been interested too. How could he help it? She was beautiful, intelligent, interested in his work, and she could cook. A man couldn't ask for more in a woman. But he knew that Reid hated the idea of his even seeing Jewel casually, and Reid had him in a hot spot. He couldn't well afford to get Reid too angry. The bastard just might produce that damned note that Mitch had so foolishly signed and have him arrested and hanged for the murder of Duncklee.

He did think, though, that he could easily get away with continuing to be just friendly with Jewel, just enough to keep Reid on edge, to needle him. He enjoyed doing that. It gave him the sense of having at least a little revenge on Reid for what the man was holding over him, but he didn't really enjoy doing it at Jewel's expense. How, he asked himself, could a no-good son of a bitch like Reid have such a lovely daughter?

"Thanks for inviting me," he said. "The supper was real good. About the best I've ever had."

"Thank you," she said. "I'm glad you liked it."

Mitch felt a little uneasy at the coziness of the situation. "The night's starting in to get a chill," he said. "I'd better not be keeping you out any longer."

He stood up as if to go.

"Wait a few minutes," she said.

Mitch sat back down. He felt really nervous now. He thought that he knew what she wanted. He knew for sure that he wanted it too, but he told himself that he couldn't allow it to happen. It was just too dangerous. Maybe, if he could somehow get that damn paper away from Reid, maybe one of these days things would be different.

"I'll be going to work in the morning," she said.

"Where at?" he asked her.

"Up at the mine," she said. "Daddy's never found a replacement for Howard Jones—or whatever his name really was. I can do the job, and I've been trying to talk him into it ever since—well, ever since Jones was killed. Well, I finally succeeded."

"It's a bookkeeping job, ain't it?" Mitch asked her.

"Yes," she said, "and I've been trained for that. I've

worked as a bookkeeper before. Not here. Before we came to Paxton.''

"You really want to work like that?'' Mitch asked her.

"Yes,'' she said. "I do.''

"Then I'm glad for you,'' he said.

They sat for a moment in silence, the night chill biting a little deeper.

"Mitch?'' she said.

"What?''

"Why did you stop me and Daddy from saying any more about what you found out?''

"What?'' he said.

"This morning,'' she said, "when Jasper was with us. Why did you stop us from saying anything more?''

"Did I do that?'' he said.

"Yes,'' she said. "You know you did. You did it twice. Why?''

"Oh,'' he said. "I don't know. Just a feeling, I guess. I thought maybe it would be best if we kept it to ourselves for a while yet. That's all.''

"You don't think that Jasper . . .''

"I don't think anything,'' he said. "It was just a feeling, like I said. That's all.''

She stood up. "You were right,'' she said. "It is getting cold. And I think you should be home in bed. You were already exposed to the cold too long the other night. And you still need your rest. Will I see you in the morning at Ellie's?''

"I reckon so,'' he said. "Good night, and thanks again.'' He turned then to walk away, but just as he got to the bottom porch step, she stopped him.

"Mitch.''

It seemed to Mitch that there was almost a desperation in her voice. He turned around, anxious in spite of himself, to hear what it was she wanted to say to him. She stood on the porch looking down at him. "Good night,'' she said. He knew that she had wanted to say more. And he had wanted to hear it. He started walking back to his combination office and home.

The streets were still busy, mostly with customers of the several tent saloons coming and going. A few men who had consumed a bit too much alcohol were staggering their uncertain ways somewhere, but they appeared harmless to Mitch. He didn't bother with them. He glanced into the saloons as he passed them by, and things seemed pretty much as they should be. All in all, he thought, it was a pretty quiet night—for Paxton. He made it back to his office without having spoken to anyone, without having had to deal with any problems.

Mitch sat up most of the night, thinking deep and conflicting thoughts. They were troubling thoughts. He had thought until recently that he had only one real problem in Paxton, and that was how to get himself out of Paxton. All of a sudden that was no longer the case. He thought about Jewel. He thought about the feelings he believed that she had for him, and he thought about the feelings he knew that he was having for her, feelings he had never had about any woman before in his life and that he had never even considered he would ever have. Then he added to those thoughts the harsh ones he had for her father. And even if he did not have those feelings toward Reid, he knew that Reid hated the idea of having his daughter involved in any way with a half-breed. It was a difficult situation he was in, and it was one he had no idea how to handle. He had never before felt so helpless. He tried to put those thoughts out of his mind and consider something else, something that he might be able to do something about.

Forcing his mind onto another subject, he asked himself, therefore, if he had done the right thing that morning at breakfast in quieting the two Reids when Boone was with them. He hadn't actually lied to Jewel about why he had done that. It really was just a feeling he had. Nothing more. A feeling and a pair of boots. Some scattered footprints. That was all. He wondered, though. Making a sudden decision, he

159

left his office and hurried over to the newspaper office. Radin was there working late to get out the morning paper. He looked up from his work, surprised to see Mitch coming in so late.

"Hello, Sheriff," he said. "What brings you around here at this late hour?"

"Howdy, Radin," Mitch said. "Is there still time to make a change in that story Reid gave you?"

"I might be able to do it," Radin said. "What is it you want?"

They met again for breakfast under the tent at Ellie's, the usual crowd: Mitch, Jewel, Reid, and Boone. They ordered their meals of eggs, ham, biscuits and gravy, and fried potatos. They ate, made small talk, and drank a great deal of coffee. Finished with his plate, Mitch casually tossed a copy of the morning *Gazette* on the table. The headline on the story was barely visible to the others, for Mitch had leaned an elbow on the folded paper and was rolling himself a smoke. Boone squinted at the paper with an interest he was not able to totally conceal.

"Can I see your *Gazette*?" he asked.

"Hmm?" Mitch muttered, seeming unconcerned. "Oh, sure," he said, lifting his elbow. Boone pulled the paper out from under Mitch's arm and unfolded it to read the front page. In a moment, he commented on what he had just read.

"You've figured it all out," he said.

"What's that?" Mitch asked.

"The murders," said Boone. "You've got it all figured out, according to this story here."

"Oh, yeah, well," Mitch said, "part of it, anyhow."

"Well," Boone said, "it says here that the murdered miners were all part of a gang of outlaws from Missouri. The Cook Gang, and the man we knew as Red Calhoun was really Elmer Cook. Apparently they were all here under assumed names."

"That much is right," Mitch said.

"All the gang members are dead except for that Sandy

Connors, and you suspect that he's the killer,'' Boone said. He was still holding the paper up in front of himself, as if referring to the story as he talked. "You think that he and the others had some sort of falling-out, and he killed them over it.''

"Brisket told us that Connors was the man,'' said Mitch. "He just kept the rest of the story to himself. He didn't want to get himself arrested for the bank robbery.''

"Well, then,'' Boone said, "you do know it all. All except the reason. You think that maybe Connors just got greedy and wanted all the money for himself?''

"I don't know,'' Mitch said. He took a deep drag on his cigarette.

"Well,'' Boone said, "I guess that really doesn't matter much. You know everything else about the case.''

"I don't know who Connors is,'' said Mitch, "and I don't know where the money is.''

"But according to this story,'' Boone said, "you've got a U.S. marshal coming to town who can identify Connors for you.''

"Yeah,'' said Mitch. "That's right.''

"Well, that's it, then. That'll wrap it all up,'' Boone said. He refolded the paper and put it back on the table.

"It should,'' Mitch agreed.

"I'll be damned,'' said Boone. "Well, congratulations. Good work, Sheriff. Damn good work.''

"Thanks, partner,'' said Mitch.

Mitch walked the back way to Sam Neely's stable, and he took his saddled horse out the back way as well when he left. Neely said something again about Mitch's sneaking around. This time Mitch didn't argue the point. He *was* sneaking. He rode along slowly behind the buildings clear to the lower end of town, and he lurked there in the shadows of the narrow passage between two buildings. He watched as Jasper Boone came out the front door of the rooming house in which he lived, carrying saddlebags and a small valise and wearing a six-gun strapped around his waist.

161

Mitch had never before seen Boone wearing a gun. Boone headed toward the high end of the street, toward Neely's place, Mitch figured. He waited until Boone was out of sight, then he mounted his horse and rode out onto the main road. He was headed down the mountain.

It wasn't easy to hurry down the mountain road, but Mitch moved his mount along as quickly as he could with some degree of safety. He had fallen down the mountain in one place recently. He wasn't planning to repeat the experience if he could avoid it. Along the way he passed by two riders and a wagon, all going up toward Paxton. People were still moving in to the growing boomtown. More moved in every day. Mitch wished that he could be moving out. He would be more than happy to give up his place to someone else. There was only one thing about Paxton that Mitch liked at all, one thing he would miss if he left. That was Jewel, and he knew that he wouldn't ever have her for anything more than a friend. The thought was a painful one, and it led to another. He had thought that his two friends in Paxton were Jewel and Jasper Boone.

Because of that, he felt almost guilty riding down toward the base of the mountain. He had liked Jasper Boone, had counted him as a friend. He wasn't as close a friend as Al Sieber or Tom Horn, but he was a friend. Or at least, Mitch had thought so. He hoped even now that he would be proven wrong in his assumption that Jasper was in fact Sandy Connors, but he didn't think so. The boots had been the first clue, but Jasper had played that one smooth. He had said that they looked his size, had even voluntarily tried them on and then said without hesitation that they only pinched a little. He had not seemed nervous, and he had not hesitated to show Mitch that the boots were at least a close fit. In short, he had not behaved like a guilty man would be expected to behave. So Mitch had let that one pass by—almost.

And then there were the many footprints matching the boots that he had found in the ground around the jail. Boone had explained that away too, and Mitch had accepted the explanation. It had been a good one. Then there was the murder weapon, a hammer, and the hacksaw blade that had been tossed to Dog and Hammerhead. Both were tools of Boone's trade. Boone was a carpenter. Even then, Mitch had made excuses for Boone. Anyone could have a hammer and a hacksaw, he had told himself. They were common enough hand tools.

But it was Boone's intense interest in the details of the case in just the last couple of days that had at last aroused Mitch's suspicion and caused him to add up the other small clues: his interest and the tone of his voice, the look on his face when he asked the questions and provided his own theories. All of it put together was nothing that Mitch could take to a court. It was not enough even to arrest Boone for. It was only, as he had told Jewel, a feeling. And it was an uncomfortable feeling, one that Mitch did not like having. He tried to tell himself that if he was right, if Boone really did turn out to be Sandy Connors, as Mitch was now almost certain he would, then he was not really a friend at all, never had been. He had been playing a role and getting close to Mitch, the sheriff, so he could know what was going on. That thought didn't help any, though. Mitch still felt guilty.

He asked himself what he would do if he had Al Sieber or Tom Horn or even Jewel in the same position in which he now had Jasper Boone, and the answer came quickly and easily. He would keep his thoughts to himself. If anyone else grew suspicious, he would warn the friend he thought to be guilty. He would become an accomplice to any one of those three. They were his friends. They were the people he cared most about in the whole world. Having thought that through, he realized that Jasper Boone had never been in that category.

When Mitch at last reached the bottom of the road, he looked out to see the flat plain stretching in all directions except one. He thought about continuing to ride, to head across that plain in any direction. It wouldn't matter. He wouldn't worry about where he was going. He would be satisfied to be riding free. He did not, of course. Instead, he located a place at the base of the mountain where he could hide his horse. Then he took the Winchester out of its sheath and went searching for another spot, one where he could hide himself and still see who was coming down the road. He selected a large boulder with room to get behind it. He settled down to wait.

Mitch looked up into the sky to see that the sun was nearly overhead. It was almost noon, and no one had come down the mountain road after him. Perhaps he had been wrong about Boone, or perhaps he had misread the man's actions when he saw him leaving the rooming house. He was about to give up the vigil for a lost cause when he heard something up above. He waited, listening intently. It was the sound of a horse coming down the road. He waited and watched. At last the horse and rider appeared. The man was Jasper Boone. Still Mitch waited. When Boone was within about twenty feet of the the bottom of the road, the spot where the road leveled off, Mitch cranked a shell into the Winchester's chamber and stepped out to the middle of the road. Boone halted his horse.

"Hello, Mitch," he said. "What're you doing down here?"

"Waiting for you," said Mitch. "You trying to leave town without saying good-bye?"

"I, uh, I tried to find you," Boone said. "I was going to tell you."

"You could have told me at breakfast," Mitch said.

"I hadn't made my mind up yet," said Boone. "It was a sudden decision. It just came to me that I could do a lot better for myself somewhere else. That's all. I'm glad to see you, Mitch. I didn't want to just ride off like that without saying anything to you."

"Jasper," Mitch said, "you're a goddamned liar."

"What?" Boone said.

"Or should I call you Sandy?"

"Now, wait a minute, Mitch," Boone protested. "You've got it all wrong. You're jumping to hasty conclusions here. Just because I'm leaving town—"

"Before the marshal shows up," Mitch said.

"Just because I'm leaving town," Boone went on, "you've decided that I'm your killer, that I'm that Sandy Connors. Well, you're wrong, Mitch. You're dead wrong."

"Then you won't mind riding back up to Paxton with me and waiting for the marshal to get here to back up your story," Mitch said.

"That could be a long wait," said Boone, "and I've got places to go. Listen, I've been trying to keep this friendly, but you're pushing me, Mitch. You've got nothing on me, nothing at all, and I insist that you lower that rifle and get out of my way. I'm riding on."

Mitch raised the barrel of his rifle just a bit. "You ain't going nowhere," he said, "except back to Paxton with me. Right now, unbuckle that gunbelt and drop it off to your right side. Go on."

Keeping his eyes on the muzzle of Mitch's rifle, Boone did as Mitch had instructed him.

"All right," said Mitch, "get down."

Boone swung off the left side of his horse. "I thought we were riding back to Paxton," he said.

"We will, after we rest your horse a spell," Mitch said. "Move over here." He indicated the big boulder with the end of the rifle barrel, and Boone walked on over there. Mitch went over to Boone's horse. He picked up the six-gun and holster from the dirt where Boone had dropped it, slung it over his shoulder, then moved up to the horse. He started to open the saddlebags.

"That's private property," Boone said. "You got no right to go poking around in there."

Ignoring Boone's protests, Mitch opened the flap and reached in. He came back out with a handful of bills. He glanced at them, then looked across the saddle at Boone over by the boulder. "I'd say that what you've got here is what's left of the hundred thousand," he said. "Am I right?"

As Mitch was stuffing the cash back into the saddlebag, Boone suddenly produced from somewhere a small pocket pistol, and he fired across the back of his horse at Mitch's head. The bullet came close, but it missed its mark, and Mitch dropped to the ground. He fired three rounds underneath the horse's belly. Two of them struck Boone in the chest and gut. The third hit his right thigh. The horse whinnied, stamped, and reared, and Mitch scurried away from it. Boone had slumped to the ground. He was still clutching the pocket pistol, but he was having trouble raising it up to a firing position. Mitch cranked another shell into the chamber of his Winchester and leveled the rifle at Boone once more.

"Drop it," he snapped.

Boone hesitated only an instant. He relaxed his fingers and let the pistol fall to the ground. It was still not far from his reach. Mitch, keeping his eyes on Boone, calmed Boone's horse.

"You've killed me, Mitch," said Boone. "You son of a bitch."

"You ain't dead," said Mitch, "but you'd have had a more comfortable ride back to town if you'd just gone on with me when I said."

He walked over to where Boone slumped against the boulder, reached down, and picked up the pocket pistol. Boone gave it a last longing look as Mitch tucked it into the waistband of his trousers. Then Mitch knelt beside Boone and tore at Boone's shirt to examine the bullet holes.

"I'll plug these up some," he said. "You'll make it. Tell me the truth now. You are Sandy Connors."

"I'm Sandy Connors," Boone said through a wince.

"Well, then," Mitch said, "what happened between you and the others, anyhow? How come you had to kill them all?"

Boone groaned as Mitch poked around the bullet holes. "My horse went lame," he said. "While we were running from the posse. Elmer said—that's Red, you know—Elmer said they couldn't afford to let me ride double with someone. Slow them down. He took my gun, and they left me behind—to die or get caught. I tricked them, though. I survived and got away clean. We had already planned on splitting up and meeting later at Paxton. Heard about it somewhere.

Western boomtown. So I knew where to find the bastards, and I came to get them.''

"How much of the loot do you have there in your saddle-bags?'' Mitch asked him.

"Most of it, I think,'' Boone said. "Some of the boys had been living on it, but they hadn't spent much. I didn't think they had. I found it in their shacks. All except what you got off Skip—that's Brisket. You had him in jail, so I never got to his shack.''

"I got no money off Brisket,'' Mitch said.

"Oh?'' said Boone. "Well, you better search again, part-ner. He had a share. Say, Mitch, why are you trying to patch me up, anyway? I tried to kill you—twice now. Besides, if I live, they'll just hang me, you know.''

"I'm a lawman, Jasper,'' Mitch said. "I'm supposed to bring you in alive to stand trial, if I can.''

"No one would ever have to know, Mitch,'' Boone said. "Why don't you just go ahead and finish it here? Huh?''

Mitch didn't answer that question. He finished patching Boone up as best he could, and then he figured Boone's horse was rested enough to start the return trip to Paxton. He loaded Boone back into the saddle, and they started the ride back up the mountain toward Paxton and the jail.

"We really ought to try to get ahold of that marshal,'' Reid said, "before he wastes a trip out here. We're keeping Con-nors here. They only want him for robbing a bank. We have him for murder. We'll try him here and hang him right here in Paxton.''

"That marshal will be wanting to take the money back,'' Mitch said.

"Oh, yeah,'' said Reid. "I didn't think about that. We'll just let him come on out, then. Speaking of the money, where do you suppose Brisket's share is?''

"I don't know,'' Mitch said. "Maybe I didn't search his shack good enough. I'll go back out there tomorrow and give it another look.''

"You don't have to do that, Mitch,'' Reid said. "I'll get

a few of the boys from the mine together, and we'll ride out there and give the place a thorough going-over. You deserve a few days' rest, boy. Take them."

"Whatever you say," Mitch agreed.

They were sitting in Reid's office, talking and smoking. It was early evening, and just then Jewel walked in.

"Well, baby," said Reid, "how was your first day out on the job?"

"It was good," she said. "Everything went real smooth. Hi, Mitch. What's going on here?"

"What makes you think anything's going on?" Reid asked her.

"I don't recall you two ever just sitting around over here—or anywhere else, for that matter—just to visit," she said.

"All right," said Reid. "You're right. Mitch got Sandy Connors today. It's all over."

She rushed toward Mitch, then stopped herself just short of running into him. "You got him?" she said. "That's great. Who is he? Anyone we know?"

"Jasper," said Mitch. "Jasper is Connors."

She hesitated a moment, looking startled. Then she started to speak. "Did you—"

"He took a shot at me, so I had to shoot him," Mitch said, "but he ain't dead. He's over in the jail. Doc patched him up. I reckon he'll live to hang."

"Jasper," she said. "I never suspected. You did, though, didn't you? That feeling you said you had."

"Yeah," he said. "I reckon."

"Well," she said, looking at her father, "like you said, it's over."

"There won't be much work for a sheriff around here now," Mitch said. "Just tossing a drunk in jail now and then. Anyone can do that. You sure don't need me. You think I could move on now?"

"Not a chance," Reid said.

"Well," said Jewel, sensing trouble and changing the subject, "how about supper at our house again tonight? To celebrate your success."

"I got a better idea," Mitch said. "How about I buy you a supper at Ellie's? You just got off work. You don't want to go to cooking right away."

She smiled and took Mitch's arm, and they started to leave the office. At the door, she turned back to face her father. "You coming, Daddy?" she asked him.

"No," Reid said. The scowl was back on his face. "I've still got some work to do here. I'll get something later."

CHEYENNE

VENGEANCE QUEST/ WARRIOR FURY

JUDD COLE

Vengeance Quest. When his cunning rivals kill a loyal friend in their quest to create a renegade nation, Touch the Sky sets out on a bloody trail that will lead to either revenge on his hated foes—or his own savage death.

And in the same action-packed volume . . .

Warrior Fury. After luring Touch the Sky away from the Cheyenne camp, murderous backshooters dare to kidnap his wife and newborn son. If Touch the Sky fails to save his family, he will kill his foes with his bare hands—then spend eternity walking an endless trail of tears.

___4531-1 $4.99 US/$5.99 CAN

Dorchester Publishing Co., Inc.
P.O. Box 6640
Wayne, PA 19087-8640

Please add $1.75 for shipping and handling for the first book and $.50 for each book thereafter. NY, NYC, and PA residents, please add appropriate sales tax. No cash, stamps, or C.O.D.s. All orders shipped within 6 weeks via postal service book rate. Canadian orders require $2.00 extra postage and must be paid in U.S. dollars through a U.S. banking facility.

Name_____
Address_____
City_____State_____Zip_____
I have enclosed $_____ in payment for the checked book(s).
Payment <u>must</u> accompany all orders. ❏ Please send a free catalog.
        CHECK OUT OUR WEBSITE! www.dorchesterpub.com

CHEYENNE

DOUBLE EDITION
JUDD COLE

One man's heroic search for a world he can call his own.

Arrow Keeper. A Cheyenne raised among pioneers, Matthew Hanchon has never known anything but distrust. The settlers brand him a savage, and when Matthew realizes that his adopted parents will suffer for his sake, he flees into the wilderness—where he'll need a warrior's courage if he hopes to survive.

And in the same volume...

Death Chant. When Matthew returns to the Cheyenne, he doesn't find the acceptance he seeks. The Cheyenne can't fully trust any who were raised in the ways of the white man. Forced to prove his loyalty, Matthew faces the greatest challenge he has ever known.

___4280-0 $4.99 US/$5.99 CAN

Dorchester Publishing Co., Inc.
P.O. Box 6640
Wayne, PA 19087-8640

DAN'L BOONE

MUSTANG DESERT

DODGE TYLER

Legendary frontiersman Dan'l Boone and his friend Snowshoe Hendee are making their way across the brutal Great American Desert in search of a herd of wild Spanish mustangs. They know that the horses will fetch a good price back in the Colonies—if they can get them back there alive. But the herd is the least of their worries, because a bitter enemy knows what trail Dan'l is taking, and he has fired up a fierce band of warriors to bring back Dan'l's scalp, or die trying.

___4509-5 $3.99 US/$4.99 CAN

DAN'L BOONE

DODGE TYLER

THE KAINTUCKS

The Natchez Trace is the trail of choice for frontiersmen heading north from New Orleans. But for Dan'l Boone and his small band of boatmen, the trail leads straight into danger. Lying in wait for the legendary guide is a band of French land pirates out for the payroll he is protecting. And with the cutthroats is a vicious war party of Chickasaw braves out for much more—Dan'l Boone's blood!

___4466-8 $3.99 US/$4.99 CAN

WARRIOR'S TRACE
Dodge Tyler

The Kentucky River has long been the lifeblood of American settlers near Dan'l Boone's home of Boonesborough. But suddenly it is running red with blood of another kind. The Shawnee and the Fox tribe have joined together in an unprecedented war to drive the white man out of their lands once and for all. And if Dan'l can't whip the desperate settlers into a mighty fighting force soon, he—and all of Boonesborough—might not survive the next attack.

___4421-8 $3.99 US/$4.99 CAN

DAVY CROCKETT

CANNIBAL COUNTRY

<hr />

David Thompson

Davy Crockett is driven by a powerful need to explore, to see what lies beyond the next hill. On a trip through the swamp country along the Gulf of Mexico, Davy and his old friend Flavius meet up for the first time with Jim Bowie, a man who will soon become a legend of the West—and who is destined to play an important part in Davy's dramatic life. Neither Davy nor Jim know the meaning of the word "surrender," and when they run afoul of a deadly tribe of cannibals, they know it will be a fight to the death.

___4443-9 $3.99 US/$4.99 CAN